"This may be the c＿＿＿＿＿＿＿ ＿＿＿＿ ＿＿＿＿ roots reach into a completely foreign territory—American musical theater. . . . Of course the book has a second source, and a more obvious one—the sword-and-sorcery tales by Robert E. Howard about the granddaddy of all barbarian heroes, Conan."

From the introduction by John Jakes

Only America's master storyteller could pull it off— and he has!

Fantasy by John Jakes

THE LAST MAGICIANS (1969)
MASTER OF THE DARK GATE (1970)
WITCH OF THE DARK GATE (1972)
MENTION MY NAME IN ATLANTIS (1972)

Brak the Barbarian
novels and collections

BRAK THE BARBARIAN (collection, 1968)
THE SORCERESS (1969)
MARK OF THE DEMONS (1969)
WHEN THE IDOLS WALKED (1978)
THE FORTUNES OF BRAK (collection, 1980)

MENTION MY NAME IN ATLANTIS

JOHN JAKES

BART

NEW YORK

Copyright © 1972 by John Jakes

Reprinted by arrangement with the Author

ISBN: 155785-003-8

First Bart Books edition: 1988

Bart Books
155 E. 34th Street
New York, New York 10016

Manufactured in the United States of America

AUTHOR'S INTRODUCTION TO THE NEW EDITION

This may be the only fantasy novel whose roots reach into a completely foreign territory—American musical theater.

I've always loved American musicals. And that's where the seed of MENTION MY NAME IN ATLANTIS came from; specifically, from the rowdy and riotous classic by Stephen Sondheim and Burt Shevelove, *"A Funny Thing Happened on the Way to the Forum."* To verify that, just compare the names of my characters with those in the program for any performance of the show. Even better, see the show.

Of course the book has a second source, and a more obvious one—the sword-and-sorcery tales by Robert E. Howard about the granddaddy of all barbarian heroes, Conan.

Admittedly this is a pretty strange mix for a novel. And there was an additional challenge. While I'd tried humor in some crime novels, I'd never attempted it in my science fiction or fantasy. Some satire, yes. But never knockabout farce.

So, when I wrote the outline and a couple of sample chapters, I did it for pleasure. I had little hope of finding someone to buy a combination of musical comedy, Conan parody and—where this came from, I don't remember—flying saucers.

I didn't reckon with the catholic taste and sense of humor of one of my long-time publishers, Donald A. Wollheim. First at Ace, and then under his own DAW imprint, Don published a number of my straight space-opera novels. But he liked this maverick, too. He thought the humor worked, and he took a chance.

To my surprise (and his, I don't doubt), MENTION MY NAME IN ATLANTIS survived well past its initial brief appearance in the category sections of bookstores. It lasted through several more printings and three different covers—none of which successfully caught the spirit of the novel, I thought. But then, that spirit is definitely oddball.

Ultimately the novel sold many more copies than any of my other sf or fantasy works. I don't know what that proves. But here it is back again . . . to my great delight. For that, I have to give first credit to Don Wollheim—and if you enjoy it, so do you.

JOHN JAKES

Greenwich, Connecticut
November, 1986

Prologue

I, Hoptor, write this, none other.

I write in the month of the Eager Virgin, in the year of the Warty Toad. That is, I believe those are the correct dates. In these confused times, who can say?

Still, I wish to provide an approximation of the correct moment in which this narrative is begun, for the benefit of all future historians who may seek to unravel the mystery of what befell our splendid Island Kingdom, fair Atlantis.

Now, so that there be no deceit between us, reader—for Hoptor the Vintner is an honest man if nothing else!—let me sketch, in brief, my motives for undertaking the task of setting down this chronicle.

First, it has been said—by ignorant, cheating rascals!—that I, Hoptor the Vintner, am no more than a thief, panderer, and peddler of influence of the most dubious sort. This narrative shall, perforce, prove all that false, and paint a portrait of myself neither flattering nor distorted, but only truthful: revealing me as I am—brave, resourceful, compassionate, keenly intelligent; in short, a humanitarian of the first rank.

However, as I take stylus in hand, I am moved rather more by considerations historical. For whatever else may be told about Hoptor the Vintner—by jealous, slanderous rogues!—be it known that, in my deepest of hearts, I loved our Island Kingdom with a great love, for there I was born, and there occasionally prospered. Until, of course, the unhappy events which I narrate here.

What a fair place she was, Atlantis! Rock in the blue sea! Imposing palaces! Splendid avenues! Women of the most vigorous, not to say unbridled, passion!

I digress.

Sunny skies—metaphorically!—smiled upon our Island Kingdom day without end, and it was men, not gods, who ultimately brought this happy condition to an unhappy end. Of Atlantis itself, the city-state upon the great rocky isle, little could be spoken. She was magnificent; her only unfortunate mannerism—if I may indulge in a conceit and thus personalize her—being a certain tendency to irritate the meteorological gods. Fierce sea storms lashed her with great frequency. Yet she remained safe and secure behind her mighty seawall with its system of intricate valving, of which I shall have more to say later in this thrilling account of her final days.

But as I have stressed, and here stress again, it was not the natural gods who destroyed the town of my birth, but witless men!

In this fashion I arrive at my chief motive for this telling, and that motive is, secondly, to provide a clear and unbiased account of the days of the fall.

For now that fair Atlantis has sunk into the sea, I have a feeling that all sorts of addle-brained authors—let us speak straightforwardly! crackpots!—will concoct fictions about her; pretty tales based upon some bit of misinformation or other mumbled to them by their toothless old grannies while they puled in their cribs.

On the other side of the sea, I am told—eastward—there supposedly exists just such a race of ignorant quill-mongers. I understand they are called Graeco, or Graeks, and are indolent fellows with nothing better to do, it seems, than write long treatises chock-full of spurious information. Happily, they are also weaklings. They cannot build stout ships. Therefore, fair Atlantis was never burdened with intercourse with them. Isolation upon an island-rock has its advantages!

In generations to come, however, such unscrupulous pseudo-scholars may, I fear, wax rich off the sufferings of we citizens of the Island Kingdom, and no doubt inaccuracies will spread pell-mell.

Thus I write.

And while my account will likely never be published—as if it could be, given my present odious circumstances!—at least mine will be the satisfaction of having set down the true, as opposed to the false, facts.

Therefore, roll back, o time! Part, o veils of yesterday!! Rise from the sweet illusions of the mind, o splendid and mighty kingdom of Atl—

This is writ sometime later. Growing overly excited, I broke my stylus and had to replace it with another.

In a less heated frame of mind, I now begin the account, in the month of the Eager Virgin, in the year of the Warty Toad, at a location—as far as I can tell!—some several hundred millions of miles from planet Earth.

✶ One ✶

A servant came from the house of Noxus, a pious old lecher if ever there was one, and sought me in the garden of my villa, where I was busy tending my vines.

Because of the unfortunate tendency of my waistline to increase, its size thereby rendering physical activity most difficult, my horticultural endeavors consisted of remaining seated upon a bench, a jar of wine in hand, while contemplating the undernourished stalks which twined over the arbors, as well as the few moldy-looking grapes which clustered here and there —pathetic things!—upon them. Naturally, any fool knows that good grapes cannot be raised in a walled garden on an island. But one must maintain appearances!

The servant entered the garden and said, "Hail, Hoptor."

"Hail," I answered, "and how may I be of service?"

"My master wishes to order some wine," said he, with a leer which would have distressed me had we not been safely hidden behind those selfsame high walls. One could not be too careful, considering that the graying Judges were never very sporting about the way in which a fellow turned a profit.

"Wine," I repeated. "For this evening, mayhap?"

"To be delivered after the evening meal." He winked. "Circumspectly. By dark, as it were."

Naturally I remained unruffled in the face of this seemingly peculiar request, replying in my smoothest manner, "And what vintage does noble Noxus desire?"

"He leaves that to your discretion. However, he bade me ask for a vintage which is robust, yet playfully teasing."

"Playfully teasing. Very good. Continue."

"One which is mellow at first contact—"

"Mellow at first contact," I said, writing upon a tablet. "Capital. More?"

"But with a certain delicious vigor when savored to the full."

"I have just the vintage in mind. It shall be delivered by me personally."

The servant raised a hand. "One more thing. My lord also

asks that in addition to the other qualities, it be a vintage of delicious bite."

Making lightning calculations on the nature of my current inventory, I crossed out the word I had previously written and inscribed *redhead*. We then haggled, first speaking loudly, then shouting. Aided by a brief exchange of blows, we settled upon the price of one hundred zebs. I helped the servant dress the wound I had given him during our commercial exchange —we Atlanteans are lusty bargainers!—and then I shook hands with him as he departed. Never let it be said that Hoptor is not democratic to a fault!

When he had gone, I retired to my study, one of forty-seven comfortable rooms in the villa which I had acquired several years earlier as a fruit of my profitable trade. There I considered the matter of exactly which vintage I would deliver to Noxus as soon as the sun went down.

There was truly but one choice. And while it might lead to an argumentative afternoon, still, Noxus was an important man, and none but the finest would satisfy. Sweeping all obstacles before me, I made the necessary arrangements, and at twilight loaded the cask onto my cart.

I noted a crack in the cart's axle that would have to be seen to eventually. I then hitched up my ass and set off through Atlantis' teeming streets.

From porches, doorways, and balconies, I was hailed and greeted, and I returned each greeting in kind. It was a matter of pride to me that, wherever I went in the city, I was known. Indeed, there was hardly a quarter—including the palace of His Exaltedness—with whose intimate affairs I was not familiar. Mothers and merchants, sluts and street-singers, all hallooed me as I moved along.

Pausing by a corner shrine, I was accosted by a juggler of my acquaintance who had been standing disconsolately with his balls in hand.

"What, Lemmix," said I, "not tossing the colored spheres this evening?"

With a miserable expression he showed me his hands, much bruised. "It's my wife. We had a fight and she thwacked me so hard with a broom handle that my fingers are totally numb."

"What caused this unhappy altercation?"

"Oh, we haven't been getting along at all well lately, Hoptor. I think she's taken a lover. The baker's boy. Is it my fault that I have to work nights, juggling these damn balls for a few miserable coins? Is it my fault that I come home dead tired and can't fulfill husbandly duties?"

8

"Well, old friend, we'll fix that. Take yourself to the Street of the Purple Pestles. Third shop on the right. Ask the owner to prepare a draft to rectify your unhappy condition. Such beverages are illegal, but they work."

"But I can't afford to buy so much as a jar of water, let alone a love potion!"

"The apothecary owes me a favor, Lemmix, so just hurry along. By the time the sun rises, you'll be sporting like a young stallion, and your wife will be sighing in utter contentment."

Thanking me profusely, he rushed off. As he hurried away, I called after him, "And be sure to mention my name!" He nodded and was gone.

From my position on the seat of my cart, I flicked my little whip and urged my ass forward. I was happy to have assisted Lemmix, for one never knows when, as it were, chickens may come home to roost. At such times, it's useful to be able to count an inventory of favors. A favor done is a favor owed, as they say.

A crowd of urchins soon surrounded the cart, teasing and whining for zebs. I waved them away, but one exclaimed, "What do you have in the cask, fatty?"

"Begone, you little ruffian, or I'll box your ears."

"That's Hoptor the Vintner," said another of the wretches to his comrades.

"Such a big cask for wine," commented the next.

"My client has a big thirst. And I have a big fist!"

That sent them packing, I don't mind telling you.

Near the next corner, an elderly fellow with a bald pate and sad eyes rushed from a doorway and seized my leg. "Hoptor, my friend, they're closing my shop!"

"What? Shutter the finest sausage shop in all of Atlantis? How dare they, whoever they are?"

"My license has been revoked by some bureaucrat at the palace. It's being given to the nephew of the assistant superintendent of licensing, a young numbskull who, I understand, can get no other job and knows absolutely nothing about the art of making sausages. To be thrown out of the business which I have operated for twenty years by a pack of political grafters is unendurable! My family is destitute!"

Indeed it was certainly so. From the open doorway where a lamp gleamed there issued the most unhappy of feminine wails.

"Now, Calumnos, calm yourself," I said to my friend, who had staked me to sausages in many a lean time. "Tomorrow morning, simply pay a visit to the licensing bureau. Ignore that

9

imbecile of an assistant superintendent and apply directly to the superintendent himself."

Blanching, Calumnos cried, "But I'll never be permitted in the office of so high a personage!"

"You will if you mention my name," I assured him. "Explain your grievance and you'll have your license back in a trice."

Modestly waving off his tears of gratitude, I flicked my ass and proceeded around the corner.

The evening was balmy and pleasant. A large percentage of our citizenry had come out of doors. Bully boys and babes in arms jostled one another along the cobbled ways, and a sky the color of lemons spread peacefully overhead. The sea could be heard murmuring against the mighty walls in periods when no one in the immediate vicinity was arguing, cursing, or shrieking in mortal pain. A pleasant aroma compounded of cheap perfume, roast meat, and unwashed bodies permeated the air. Unsavory to some, perhaps, but it was the scent of the life of my fair city. I relished it.

Shortly, a press prevented me from passing on with speed, so I climbed down and walked around the rear of the cart. I thought I had heard knocking. Bending close to the cask, I hissed:

"What's the matter? Can't you breathe?"

In reply, I heard only a scratching sound, then a kind of feline wailing in which I recognized but one word. That, however, was sufficient to freeze the blood, the word being *marriage*.

I precluded further discussion by rapping the cask sharply and growling, "Be quiet, we're in the midst of a small mob."

As in truth we were. Many had gathered in a little plaza, in the center of which, on a crate, stood a deranged looking woman of middle years. I realized belatedly that she was some sort of seeress, with which Atlantis is overpopulated— not to say afflicted!

Tearing her hair—a bit too vigorously for my taste!—she cried, "Doom! Doom! Doom!"

"Doom?" I said to one nearby. "What's all this about?"

"Fortuna is predicting a great calamity soon to befall th kingdom."

"Oh, is that all." It happened week in, week out.

"Yes, but two dead hogs were found in the temple last nigh Also, this morning, three sets of twins were born within a hour of each other. And all backward!"

"The former is a prank, the latter of no significance,"

10

informed him, though in truth the latter, so freighted with the overtones of matrimony, curdled my spine and sent me hurrying ahead until I, ass, and cart had mercifully bypassed the throng.

"Doom! Doom—!" The harpy's cries faded from my ears none too soon.

I had no faith in the ubiquitous street prophets. Yet I do confess to a peculiar and lingering sense of unease following the exhibition by the seeress. Of late, these prophecies of calamity had been coming with greater and greater frequency. And, in most curious fashion, fair Atlantis had been visited by few, if any, of the raging sea storms which customarily ravaged it, month in, month out.

Traders fresh off commercial ships continued to report the usual maelstroms far out to sea. But in recent weeks, the Island Kingdom had remained becalmed; as if the gods were withholding their wrath in order to make a final blow more devastating—

I am happy to report that these unwholesome broodings did not linger long, thanks to the sudden appearance of a young woman who hailed me from a second floor balcony and then came rushing down an outer stair.

That is, she rushed as fast as her noticeably distended stomach would permit!

"What's this, Rhomona? Married and starting a family? And it was only last month you were industriously engaged outside the soldiers' barracks!"

"Oh, Hoptor—ohhh!" Misery prevented her from saying more.

She was not a bad looking wench, though she lacked the wit and grace to succeed in the wine trade. She had often importuned me to take her into my vineyard, as it were. Regretfully, I had been forced to decline, familiar as I was with her bent for profanity, not to mention the aura of refinement demanded by my august clientele. Rhomona's handicaps did not prevent me from liking her, however.

"I am not married!" she wailed at last, then launched into one of those unseemly diatribes which seemed endless in their repetitive outrage; I suffered through the blistering profanities, then inquired:

"Pray, who is the object of all this wrath, girl? Some military man?"

"Oh, no, a lying, cheating—" Another passage of gutter discourse too shocking to be recorded here. Then: "He said he loved me! He said it was perfectly safe! And when I went

11

to his house, after I discovered I was in this condition, he said I should go away."

"Tell me the name of the rascal at once."

She did. I blanched.

"That is a predicament, Rhomona. Not only is he highly placed among the nobility, he is married."

"So I found out," sobbed the poor child. "Afterward! Now I can't work—"

"Yes," I agreed with heartfelt sympathy, "I can see how a customer would be a trifle loath to snuggle up to—yes, I see the problem."

"Kindly Hoptor—" She tried to bring herself close to the cart, but the protrusion of her abdomen made this difficult. She settled for straining on tiptoes and grasping my hands. "Is there nothing that can be done to force the father of my unborn child to pay his just due?"

"Unfortunately, I doubt it. Not only is the gentleman you named of high station"— (Why had he not come to me for a vintage? I wondered, with some pique.) —"but his wife, a shrew in every respect, is none other than the intimate confidante of Her Exaltedness, Voluptua. Attempting to blackmail folk of that sort will only land you in the king's dungeons."

"But I won't be able to work for months! I'll starve!"

"Not if you get a short loan, my dear."

"Pay the usurious rates of those vile moneylenders? Forty percent? I'll be repaying them the rest of my life! No, Hoptor, I simply can't."

"You certainly can," I returned with confidence, "provided you visit only the moneylender I have in mind. Graspus, at number eighteen, Covet Lane. Do you know the location?"

At her pathetic nod, I continued, "Present yourself at his door this very night, mention my name, and borrow what funds you need. But pay not one zeb over four percent. If he grows testy, simply say that Hoptor the Vintner has not forgotten the matter of the lady barber with the freckles."

"The freckles? The freckles where?"

"Graspus knows where. Now take yourself along, girl, and speedily."

Murmuring, "The lady barber with freckles," and pausing in between these murmurs to heap gratitude upon my head, she disappeared with what I must admit was a highly comical waddle.

And after she was gone, the air was noticeably fresher. The unfortunate creature had an aversion to soap, no doubt due

12

to her coarse upbringing. Despite her now-bloated charms, she would simply never be welcome in my vineyard. However, I was delighted to have assisted her, particularly since Graspus was a bad sort anyway, and needed to be reminded from time to time of his perverse antics with the lady barber.

As a result of my various encounters with the citizens of the street, I was falling behind in my delivery schedule, and now hastened to catch up. I drove my ass at a rapid clip, ignoring many unsettling creaks and snaps from the cart axle. In similar fashion, I paid little heed to the bumps and thumps issuing repeatedly from the interior of the large cask. My vintage, it seemed, was growing equally aware of the many delays.

I drove on through the darkening streets, as lamps began to gleam in the apartments of Atlantis. But, as it turned out, swift passage to the abode of Noxus was not decreed by the fates.

Once more I was confronted by a press of citizenry, this three times larger than the one which had gathered to hear the rantings of the seeress. The way ahead was totally blocked. I was in process of turning my ass's head around to take a different route down an alley—in short temper, I don't mind telling you!—when I recognized the spindly figure with the long white beard clinging to the fountain, haranguing the mob.

"The government is corrupt! Yonder in the great palace, its figureheads loll in indolence, while we, the long-suffering citizens of Atlantis, pay the penalty. The rulers may ignore the populace at their peril! Dire times are coming! Have you not all heard that a dead hog was found in the temple only last evening?"

"Three dead hogs!" someone cried.

"No, it was two," I exclaimed in some irritation to the last speaker, who was standing directly in front of my ass, impeding further movement. "Will you kindly step aside so that I may turn my cart around?"

"You heard it, citizens!" shrilled the old man. "Four dead hogs. And triplets born backward with cauls this very day! Those are not the only portents, either. Constantly, we are warned of the utter inadequacy of those who presume to call themselves our betters! I have seen heavenly discs flashing in the very sky which arches above us—surely a sign that the gods are displeased!"

In truth, I was more intrigued by this discourse than I had been by the outpourings of the seeress, for the speaker in this

13

case was a person of some note. My ass, however, balked in its efforts to answer my tugs on the reins and, not remotely interested in accounts of omens and portents, took matters into its own jaws, as it were. It stretched its head forward to the citizen who refused to move, and bit his backside.

Pulling a dirk, the man shrieked, "Come down from that seat, you fat baboon, and you'll see that you can't get away with that sort of thing!"

Unsettled I answered, "I am not responsible for the actions of my animal, sir."

"We'll see about that!" the fellow returned, approaching me with menacing motions of his knife. All at once, thank the gods. several others in the throng came to my assistance, exclaiming variously:

"Leave him alone, you lout!"

"That's Hoptor the Vintner, don't you recognize him?"

"Trifle with Hoptor and we'll split your head open."

In the gloom, I failed to recognize those who spoke, but doubtless I had assisted them at some point in the past, as I had assisted others this same evening. Indeed, I would wager that fully eighty percent of the citizens of fair Atlantis were in my debt in some fashion, and I was a popular figure, if I say so myself. The various snarls and growls cowed the bully boy. With a last oath, he put up his knife, while I congratulated myself once again upon my philosophy of always being of service to my fellow man by means of my wide acquaintance with nearly every facet of street life and commerce. When one mentioned the name of Hoptor the Vintner, one conjured with a true talisman!

"—our king. Geriasticus X, is simple and ineffectual. His queen, Voluptua, is scandalous and depraved. Together, they govern ill, and thus invite the wrath of the gods, which we have seen recently manifested in the increasingly frequent portents—"

I lost much of the rest of it, for curious though I might be, I could no longer delay reaching the house of Noxus. At the same time, the crowd continued to grow, for as I have suggested, the speaker, Babylos, was a man of note. Of noble birth, he had once been considered the Island Kingdom's foremost scholar. He studied the stars, assaulted convention, and pulled down popular idols at every opportunity. Now. in his senility, his outpourings concerning "heavenly discs" and other occult visions had grown familiar. While no one quite took the poor old scarecrow seriously, he yet managed to attract considerable attention.

"—I tell you, citizens, our rulers are so corrupt that we shall inevitably suffer the fury—"

Screams, outcries, and other alarms indicated that the gathering was about to be interrupted, to no good end for Babylos. I spied the gleam of armor, heard the tramp of boots along a nearby street. Babylos would learn to speak against the government in public!

But I confess I was less concerned for him than for my own person, especially considering the vintage in the cask which creaked back and forth on the bed of my cart.

Carrying torches and shouting, "Hup, hup!" in that mindless fashion of theirs, the soldiers marched into the far side of the crowd, causing additional outcries and general consternation.

Immediately I recognized their leaders, including General Pytho, in person, and at his side his toady, Captain Num. Both were highly unpopular with the masses. Pytho was His Exaltedness' commander-in-chief, which bespoke the importance the palace laid on silencing the voice of Babylos. That, in turn, testified to the general shakiness of the throne.

"Haul the wretch down from there!" General Pytho commanded.

"Yes, we'll teach you to cry treason in the streets, you dog," squealed Captain Num, himself a dog trained to bark at his master's every twitch.

Torches flared, swords flashed, the soldiers broke cadence to shove forward in the crowd in a boorish fashion, and I abandoned philosophic speculations on why the crowned heads should be so concerned about the rantings of one doddering old astrologer. The presence of Pytho and Num had intensified my desire to be away from the vicinity, and I lost no time in maneuvering my ass into position for a speedy flight back up the street by which I had arrived.

✳ Two ✳

Happily for me, the crowd began to hiss, boo, and pelt the soldiers with offal and decayed fruit peelings. Very shortly,

15

the entire street seemed to be in motion, all persons swaying back and forth like waves, a queasy effect, I don't mind admitting. But it was a useful distraction.

On the balconies on both sides of the thoroughfare, citizens drawn by the clamor added their shrill abuse to that of the crowd around the fountain. It certainly seemed that the gods were smiling on my head, for my actions went totally unnoticed. I had my ass half turned around, and would shortly be flogging it back around the first corner, to safety.

Babylos refused to be intimidated by the thicket of spears and swords, shouting, "The voice of truth and freedom shall not be stilled by force!"

That shows you how much he knew. Captain Num fought his way to the fountain's base, seized the old man's long beard and tugged ferociously. With a shriek, Babylos toppled from sight.

The soldiers surged forward. I heard the unhappy clink of chains, signifying the old nobleman's imminent incarceration.

Having turned my ass full around, I laid on the little whip. The faithful beast leaped forward so precipitously that I was all but bounced from the seat. I wished to depart speedily, but not that speedily!

The cart bounced and banged over the cobbles while I struggled to check my ass's mad flight. At that point, the gods saw fit to withdraw their favor.

No doubt overstrained by the severe jouncing, the axle whose dangerous condition I had noted earlier cracked completely.

The cart descended to the street. I fell off, striking the roadway with an impact which left me dizzy. My terrified ass sat down on its rump, and I perceived a second, crunching crash whose source, in my addled state, I did not immediately identify.

Tottering to my feet, I applied my lash to the ass's flanks. "Forward, forward, you wretch!"

Some of my acquaintances on the balconies were amused at my plight. Among other impolite rejoinders, I heard, "Hoptor, get a horse!"

I flashed a glance toward the fountain. The crowd continued to surge back and forth, shouting and hissing at the military, who in turn menaced the populace with their weapons. In the throng I glimpsed the ornate helmets of Pytho and Num, but of Babylos there was no sign. The soldiers hadn't spied me yet, but I didn't intend that they should. I began to berate my ass and box its ears with my fists.

16

"Ooo, look, Hoptor's cask has sprung a leak!"

"Hoptor old boy, where'd you find that juicy vintage?"

"Can I press that little grape, Hoptor you sly fox?"

These and similar hoots caused me to recognize—belatedly!—the source of that second crash. In utter horror, I cried:
"Aphrodisia! Get back in the barrel!"

That will illustrate my state of mind, for of course the poor girl could do no such thing, the cask having rolled off the cart and broken apart, releasing her from its confines.

Her matchless red hair and her sparkling blue eyes were all aglow—flames to illumine my guilt, as it were! And her splendid, not to say maddening, figure was hardly concealed by the diaphanous girdle and metal bosom-cups in which she had attired herself for delivery to Noxus. If this were not calamity enough—my vintage standing in plain sight amid the wreckage of the cask!—the ungrateful minx was crying crocodile tears:

"Hoptor you villain (*sob*), I'll (*sob*) have no more!"

I rushed to her side. "Aphrodisia! Beloved! Please be quiet!"

Lovely to look at, and at the same time the very picture of feminine wrath, she stamped her beautiful little foot. "Beloved? Hah! This is the end, Hoptor, the absolute end. I've never stayed in one of those filthy casks such a long time. I thought I would die of suffocation!"

"Kindly control yourself," I whispered with some urgency. "Take note of your surroundings!"

"I'll shout it from the highest roof of the temple!" she exclaimed. "I'm sick of this sort of life. Sick, sick, sick!"

In an effort to convey the seriousness of the situation, I mouthed the word *soldiers* while hooking a thumb in the direction of the fountain. So far, we had escaped the attention of all but those nearest us in the crowd. But how long could luck hold good, with the citizens on the balconies calling down jests at my expense and rushing indoors to summon their friends to the spectacle?

The trouble with Aphrodisia, you must understand, is that she was a fine girl but a bad vintage.

"I (*sob*) don't know why I've put up with it (*sob*) this long!"

"Please, dear," I pleaded, "let's discuss it in private."

"No, I refuse. I'm bruised all over from that unmerciful ride and I demand an answer. Hoptor, when are you going to marry me?"

"Gods!" I raged. "Can't you see that this is entirely the wrong time to discuss such an intimate subject?"

"Oh, you always have some excuse with which to put me

off! Oh, you're such a wicked man! Oh, I wish I didn't care for you so!"

Her last words were delivered with what I can only describe as a wail. As she proclaimed them, she flung her arms around me and burrowed her head against my shoulder, which immediately felt as though it had been rained upon. I was in quite a state, I don't mind telling you.

True, I felt a deep affection for Aphrodisia—even love, who could say? But I had been reared by ceaselessly wrangling parents. And the specter of wedded bliss was second only in my mind to disemboweling at the hands of master torturers. Thus I fobbed off Aphrodisia with every cenceivable excuse; I would make an unhealthy husband because I was too fat; I was a person of bad character engaged in a criminal trade; I was too old for her. All were true in various degrees, including the last. She was in her tender twentieth year. I was a decade and a half her senior.

To my sorrow, however, on a number of occasions I had impetuously promised to marry her in order to gain her continued cooperation. She refused to understand that one promised many people many things in order to succeed!

"You promised, Hoptor! You swore we'd be wed!"

"And we shall, my dearest, we shall! But let's not settle the mundane details here. I know a tavern nearby. Over a cup of wine—"

"Stop pulling me that way. You just want to get me drunk so I'll forget the whole thing."

"Oh, go ahead and marry her, Hoptor," suggested a man on a balcony. "You're not getting any younger."

"No time like the present," chimed in another. "Why, we can fetch a priest and stage the ceremony right here."

"With the General and his sweetheart for witnesses!" brayed a third.

I was torn between importuning the wailing girl and casting alarmed glances toward the fountain, for Aphrodisia's noise had succeeded in attracting much unwelcome attention. Babylos, no doubt already hustled off in irons, was forgotten as various members of the throng turned in our direction. Death and damnation!

"Aphrodisia, my little darling, *unless we get out of here—*"

"Not before we get things straight! I'm tired of being a—a common slut. I want to be an honest, respectable woman."

"You'll be a prison inmate if you're not careful," I retorted. She paid absolutely no attention.

"I've suffered you to hire me out to those dreadful old men

18

you call clients (*sob*) only because I wanted to please you (*sob*), in the hope you would honor (*sob*) your promise. But I'll delay no longer. You'll marry me, or—"

"Oh-oh," I said, "now you've done it!"

For mad-eyed Babylos had not yet been hustled away, but was, in fact, just this moment being hauled to jail, his wrists and ankles manacled. The soldiers were bringing him at quick step up the very street where I stood with Aphrodisia, trapped in circumstances which, to my mind, had all the aspects of a bad dream.

At the head of the procession marched General Pytho and that sissy Num. The latter was first to spot us.

"Look, General, it's the Vintner!"

Both halted without giving any signal. Their soldiers behind collided with one another, causing much stumbling and cursing while General Pytho digested the situation, then strutted forward.

The general was a swart, thick-armed man who had to have his armor specially forged in order that it accommodate his swollen belly. Hoptor the Vintner might be called fat, but certainly my excess weight was more pleasingly distributed!

Pytho's pug face displayed a horrid collection of scars, which many of the uninformed attributed to stiff military combat. I, for one, was fully aware that the rogue had schemed his way to power, had never seen battle, and had acquired his unwholesome appearance from the dirks and clutching hands of other officers whom he had stabbed or strangled in order to remove them from his way. He had, in short, climbed to his station as supreme commander over the corpses of fellow soldiers unfortunate enough to trust him.

If that weren't enough, Pytho was a man of unappetizing personal tastes, witnessed by the fact that his aide and confidante, Captain Num, looked more like a pretty girl than a soldier. To see Num mincing along in breastplate and greaves while batting his curled eyelashes and pursing his pomaded lips certainly lent credence to the contention of those who, like Babylos, argued that the imperial government of fair Atlantis had become rotten to the core.

All this information, needless to say, did not pass through my brain at that particular time. In fact, I was solely concerned with my vulnerable position.

"Well, well," said Pytho, "the Vintner indeed. We've had our eye on you a long time, fellow."

"But now we've caught the pandering wretch with the evidence!" squealed Num, waving a nicely manicured hand at

Aphrodisia. I must say that she had finally been shocked into realizing the error of her ways. Once too often she had harangued me about marriage, and she now knew full well that her caterwauling had thrust us into a situation of dire peril. Her blue eyes fairly burned with fright. My heart bled for her only a little less than it did for myself.

"Pandering?" I replied, putting up an indignant front. "Of all the base, ill-founded, ridiculous accusations—!"

"Oh, come on, Hoptor," Pytho barked. "Everyone in Atlantis knows you're the number one peddler of high quality flesh."

"Scandalous lies!"

"And as the protector and guardian of public morals—"

"Outrageous calumny!"

"—I am delighted to place you and your baggage under arrest."

Oaths and jeers from the crowd in the street and on the balconies greeted this sententious announcement. I continued to protest my innocence, but was drowned out by the catcalls echoing from every hand:

"Come off it, beefy! Public morals indeed!"

"The pot's calling the kettle black!"

"How are your morals when you're holding hands with your captain?"

"Silence!" General Pytho screamed, flourishing his sword in a menacing way. All his facial scars turned purple simultaneously. "I'll have every one of you on the gibbet if this insolence continues!"

"I've never been so insulted in my life," pouted Captain Num.

His eyes fired by a frenzy for justice, old Babylos rattled his chains and shook his fists. "Fly, Hoptor! Fly, Aphrodisia! Fly from the hands of these authoritarian brutes!"

"That's enough out of you," said Pytho, whacking Babylos aside the head with the flat of his sword. The old nobleman groaned and collapsed in a heap. The general gestured at me and my vintage. "Soldiers, chain these two!"

Spears and blades at the ready, Pytho's thugs rushed forward. It was a tense moment, I don't mind stating. But once again, my care in cultivating my position as benefactor to common citizens of Atlantis came to my aid. In the mob, and on the balconies, Babylos' cry was repeated many times:

"Fly, Hoptor!"

"Fly, Aphrodisia!"

"Fly from the scum!"

To lend assistance, those above straightaway began to make things difficult for the soldiers by throwing down whatever was at hand: wine jars, vases of flowers, furniture, the contents of slop pots, and hot charcoal from braziers. Those in the street began to trip and punch the soldiers, and in a twinkling, a furious melee had developed, against which the weapons of Pytho's brutes could not prevail.

Being nearer the advancing soldiers than I was, Aphrodisia stretched out her hands to implore assistance. It is not true, as some have claimed, that I shouted, "Fend for yourself!" No, there is a much more human explanation to my subsequent behavior.

I knew the unfortunate girl was much more likely to be caught by the troops than was I. Thus it seemed sensible to retain my own freedom of movement, in order to assist her at some time in the future. Therefore, I turned and ran.

A soldier lunged at me. Nimbly, I clambered over my ass, whom the militaristic pig, attempting to hit me, inadvertently jabbed with his spear. The ass reared up. Its hind legs flew out. The soldier shot backward, victim of hooves in the mouth.

By that time, dodging a rain of refuse, burning coals, potted plants, and taborets, I had gained the shelter of a nearby alley.

"After him, after him!" Captain Num could be heard squealing.

Unaccustomed to vigorous exercise, I soon developed piercing pains in my chest. But I ran on with every ounce of stamina at my command, reminding myself that I was fleeing for Aphrodisia, and Aphrodisia alone. The poor girl was now a prisoner, and someone must see to her freedom!

Presently, in a semi-delirious state, I halted in a darkened street and panted for air. The clamor was still audible, but distantly. I knew the back ways of Atlantis better than most of the troops, certainly. I had eluded them by taking advantage of that fact.

But I remained in a state of nerves as I took a circuitous route to my villa, climbed the garden wall—with considerable effort!—and ultimately locked myself in the wine cellar. There I opened a fresh jar, as a stimulant to thinking, and congratulated myself upon being free to help my beloved.

After I had drunk the entire jar of wine, it still seemed to me that cerebral functions were operating slowly. Therefore I drank another jar. In the midst of the third, I made the happy discovery that I was at last in a frame of mind to plan my strategy.

21

The clever reader may be wont to inquire as to why, in order to ply my trade, I indulged at all in the elaborate charade of wines, casks, and vintages. The reasons are shamelessly simple.

I operated on a much higher plane than did, let us say, the unsavory fellows who sneak through the streets drumming up business for the likes of poor pregnant Rhomona. Due to my methods, my girls—my vintages!—enjoyed a preferred position. They were able to live in comparative luxury, occupying spacious, airy apartments in the most refined parts of town. They ventured out only when I summoned them. Thus they suffered far less risk than the common wenches of the street. Little Rhomona had been arrested more times than I cared to count.

Further, my role as "vintner" protected my clients, all men of the finest lineage. And the novelty of selecting a "vintage" appealed, frankly, to the tastes of the bored intelligentsia. It appealed to me as well. One does not care to be branded with unwholesome names such as "panderer."

Finally, I did not see my occupation as such a great crime, for I was only servicing natural instincts and urges which would be appeased by another, were I not to leap into the breach. I considered the oppressive cruelties and the unnatural recreational preferences of a General Pytho far more scurrilous than my well-run service to the gentlefolk.

Of course, I'd had scrapes with the law, in the persons of the dour, hair-splitting old political hacks who served as the Judges of the Island Kingdom. They—frustrated spoilsports to a man!—considered my activities illegal. Until now, however, I had always managed to avoid prosecution, largely because of my multitudinous connections with this or that individual of influence.

Tonight was a different matter.

Why, oh why, had Aphrodisia chosen that precise moment to discuss my promises of marriage? The calamity which had befallen us was, I reckoned in my clear-headed state, sometime during consumption of a fourth jar of wine, all her fault.

Was I to be held responsible because silly young girls can think of nothing except marriage, babies, and an eternity of what they imagine to be domestic bliss, but which is, in reality, unpleasantness alternating with ennui of the most crashing sort?

Was I to be faulted if such unrealistic attitudes necessitated, on my part, a few little white lies to make things run smoothly?

I certainly didn't want Aphrodisia to retire from my vineyard. Quite apart from the fact that I was fond of her—that fondness definitely stopping short of matrimony, it must be reaffirmed!—she was in great demand among the gentlemen of quality. Losing her would have halved my gross!

Nevertheless, I had lost her tonight. And in my present frame of mind, I was inclined to let the vexatious little baggage stew in her own juices.

Let her spend a holiday in the dungeons of Geriasticus X! I thought. That will make her life with me seem paradise on Earth!

A vigorous knocking abovestairs forestalled further consideration of the matter. I doused the lamp, finished the jar at hand, and, while the soldiers battered at my front gate, crying ugly oaths and waving lanterns, I crept through the house by a route known only to myself. I paused only long enough to seize a cloak and a dirk. Once more I went over the garden wall, to the safety of the street.

Darkness had fallen complete. It was late, most lamps extinguished. In the wine cellar, I had been thinking clearly. Here in the chilly air, it seemed that a strange intoxication gripped my senses. I found myself actually feeling sorry for Aphrodisia's plight. Not to mention responsible!

Certainly I must have been out of my head to distort the facts of the situation to the point where I felt I must take steps to help her. But distort them I evidently did, for shortly I was making my way to the seamiest quarter of town. Rotten Row, as it was called.

Halfway there, a pathetic cutpurse tried to rob me. When he saw who it was that he had attempted to victimize, he fell on his knees to beg my pardon. I told him to go to a certain house in one of the better sections and mention my name to the steward, whereupon he would be given a free meal and, if he so desired, honest employment.

The former appealed to the would-be thief, but the latter caused him to tremble and rush away. I passed on, concluding that one's philanthropic activities do not always meet with success.

The Bloody Bench was the most unsavory of all the unsavory dives along Rotten Row. I was recognized the moment I stepped into its furious din. But I was not molested by the assortment of head-wallopers, sharps, harlots, and roughnecks assembled in the stygian gloom. Summoning the landlord, I asked that a jar of wine be sent to my table on tab. Then I inquired if he had a lad available.

"Aye, Hoptor, I think little Mimmo's back. For some reason, purse-lifting is slow tonight."

"So I've discovered."

Little Mimmo proved to be a handsome child of seven, with a bloodied dagger in his belt and the eyes of a wolf. I told him where and how to proceed, making sure he understood that he was to apply to the night warden of the king's dungeon, and mention my name. In two hours, Mimmo returned with his report:

"Begging the gentleman's pardon—"

"Oh, what's that?"

"Sleepin' a nat, sir?"

"Thinking, my little man, thinking!"

"Well, she ain't in the prison, that's for sure."

"What, Aphrodisia not locked up? Where is she, then?"

"She ain't in the regular prison," Mimmo emphasized. "Your fren' the night warden has got her in a special cell. He says he'd like to help you sneak her out, too, but 'cause of this special cell business, he can't. It'd mean his head if he was caught."

"Perfectly understandable. Continue."

"Accordin' to what he told me, General Pytho's goin' to send her to the slave mart tomorrow, an' sell her. Your fren' said the general remarked that the gel was fair enough to bring a top price. In fac', he said she was fair enough to take to his own bed. Then some captain began weepin', and the general changed his mind."

I thwacked the table with my fist. "That unscrupulous villain! The very highest military officer in the kingdom turns a personal profit from Aphrodisia's misfortune. That shows you how rotten this state's become! Perhaps Babylos is right."

The lynx-eyed lad professed a thirst after I paid him, so I told him to speak to the landlord, in my name. Shortly little Mimmo was seated on the lap of a jolly whore, tickling her and swilling it down with the best of them.

Safe from the molestations of the hypocritical forces of law and order, I continued to drink at the Bloody Bench for the remainder of the night—in order to facilitate clear thinking!

Unfortunately, no amount of clear thinking would remove the compelling certainty that, on the morrow, I would have to visit the slave mart, to see what could be done about rescuing Aphrodisia before she was sold into bondage—to someone else!

✳ Three ✳

Shortly after daybreak, I returned to my villa. I was relieved to discover no soldiers in the neighborhood. I entered without difficulty, prepared my customary light breakfast of a dozen eggs, half a hock of ham, a loaf of bread, and a jar of wine, and thereafter sought the closet in which I kept my long, dark cloak with voluminous cowl.

Making certain that the cowl concealed my features, I took myself to the mart, which was a spacious plaza immediately behind the buildings that housed the governmental water works.

The bureaucrats who oversaw the Island Kingdom's massive seawall and maintained its intricate valving system—designed so as to drain away excess water at once, in the event fair Atlantis was ever visited by a tidal wave which rose above the wall proper—these bureaucrats, I say, were already scurrying to work, carrying their noontime snacks in oilskin bags. Despite my predicament, I counted myself lucky to be an entrepreneur, rather than one of those lackluster fellows chained by circumstance to shuffling stone tablets back and forth across a marble desk.

The slave mart consisted of a large auction block in the center of the plaza, and a separate building at one side of the square which contained the pens and the manager's office. To the latter I repaired at once, noting the crowd already assembled, even though the bargaining would not begin for several minutes.

As I stepped into the seamy hall, I heard the inevitable lamentations from the unhappy souls confined in the cells at the rear. Intermixed were the weepings of children, the babblings of senile grannies doubtless clapped into bondage for failure to pay debts, and some drunken wretch howling a maudlin ballad about his faraway homeland in Nubia, where no one was ever discouraged, and the skies were not cloudy, sunrise to sunset. A piece of sentimental twaddle if I ever heard one!

I bypassed a number of the mart's juvenile helpers who were indolently pitching zebs at a line on the floor, and entered the main office. The manager was a burly fellow of long acquaintance. Reading a memorandum inscribed on a tablet, he glanced up as I entered. I told him that I wished to make arrangements to purchase on credit.

"No credit, stranger," he growled. "All sales are zebs on the barrelhead."

"Surely that only applies to poor credit risks," said I, whipping aside my cowl to allow him a flash of my features.

"Hoptor! Why didn't you mention that it was you?"

"Ssh!" I replied, concealing my face instantly. "I don't want my name mentioned because I happen to be in disfavor with the authorities."

His brows shot up. "Oh yes, I believe I did hear something to that effect. Is that why one of your girls goes on sale this morning? And why you're here?"

"A brilliant deduction! Is Aphrodisia on the premises?"

"She certainly is. Pytho's little sweetheart, Captain Num, brought her down an hour ago."

"Is he on the premises?"

"No, he bade me deliver the proceeds of the sale to the general when the auction's over. Then he left."

"That avaricious scoundrel!"

"Captain Num?"

"General Pytho!"

In terse syllables, I highlighted the developments of the preceding evening. At the conclusion, the manager glumly agreed that the general's pretension of enforcing the law, coupled with his attempt to make a personal gain from Aphrodisia's bad luck, was a sorry circumstance indeed. I said:

"That's why I've vowed to buy her back, much as it pains me to part with the zebs."

"Well, Hoptor, your credit's good with me anytime."

"Thanks. Just make sure your auctioneer doesn't mention my name during the bidding. I don't want to attract undue attention until the notoriety dies down. In a few days, General Pytho will be off riding some new hobbyhorse, and it will be safe for me to appear in public again. In the meantime, the auctioneer must refer to me only as the gentleman in the cloak."

"Gentleman—? Oh, of course. I'll make a note of that."

He did, on a tablet. Then he shook my hand. When I asked him what that was for, he replied:

"Why, I'm wishing you luck, Hop—sir. Your little—ah—

vintage is a choice one, if I do say so. The bidding is liable to be spirited. I certainly hope you're the one who walks away with the prize."

With visions of bankrupting myself in order to obtain Aphrodisia's freedom flashing in my head, I retired to the plaza to await the start of the sale. How much would she cost me?

I confess, in the privacy of this narrative, that I was tempted to forget the whole thing. She wasn't the only fish in the sea. But my natural fondness for the wench, plus my innately humanitarian nature, prevailed.

The crowd swelled to more than two hundred before the auctioneer appeared. A few small benches were provided for bidders on a first come, first serve basis. I noted the occupants of these, and finally moved in on a grandfather who could be no less than eighty. His arms were mere matchsticks. Unlike some of the robust types occupying other benches, he was the very picture of feebleness.

I told the old fellow that he was wanted in the manager's office. He doddered away. When he returned to find me seated, a few flourishes of my fist convinced him not to start an altercation. He went off grumbling, while I congratulated myself upon my sagacity as well as my comfort.

The auctioneer, a lascivious fellow in a breechclout, mounted the block and began to strut up and down, cracking his whip to gain everyone's attention.

"Good morning, ladies, good morning, gents. Welcome to the finest display of human flesh offered for your approval and purchase this side of the Pillars. Madam, please take that child out of the first row, some of our captives have been known to leap down and flail the audience with their chains."

After another crack of his whip, he continued, "All merchandise is offered strictly as is. However, the management guarantees that the various persons on sale are of reasonably sound health, and will not expire within seven days of purchase, or your money back."

A boy ran up with a tablet which the auctioneer consulted.

"The first item this morning is a double measure of nocturnal pleasure. Two deliciously feminine creatures who have voluntarily turned themselves into bondage in order to pay their father's gambling debts and subsequent funeral expenses. May I present the Zecchi sisters!"

Two mole-decorated middle-aged horrors were dragged from the building in chains. They made General Pytho appear a veritable god of slimness. The Zecchi sisters simpered at the

27

crowd and lifted their skirts to show off their overstuffed thighs. I, for one, rolled my eyes to heaven.

To my amazement, however, the senile old man whom I had displaced from the bench bought them at once and, giggling lewdly, led them away. There is simply no accounting for taste.

Several runaway soldiers came next. I couldn't blame them for having tried to escape. Who would want to muster under a rogue like Pytho? Since the fellows were all well built, bidding was animated. They were soon purchased by the owner of the largest sewer engineering firm in fair Atlantis. They seemed happy about it, too.

Next came a family whose wrecked skiff had left them penniless on our rocky shore. My attention wandered.

Bemused, I was not aware of the new arrival until he thrust against me, having seated himself on my bench, which was designed to hold but one person.

"This seat is taken!" I snarled.

"What did you say, pork-guts?"

I could barely reply, "Why—ah—I said, always room for one more!"

The man had seated himself so close to me that I was virtually forced off my end of the bench. There I hung precariously in space, only a fraction of my hindquarters having any support at all. Maintaining my equilibrium became a constant struggle.

The rude fellow who had placed me in this undignified position was a forbidding, not to say remarkable, specimen. He was young, with eyes of brighter blue even than Aphrodisia's. A mane of yellow hair reached well below his shoulders.

A patchwork cloak of moldy animal skins hung down his back, secured at his throat by a chain decorated with animal claws as long as my middle finger. A hide clout, fur boots, and numerous dented metal arm rings—junk jewelry if I ever saw it!—completed his ensemble.

The lout's mammoth broadsword, unsheathed, kept gouging my hip. He appeared unconcerned, scowling at the auction block in a most disagreeable way. The great brute was certainly not unhandsome. But his expression was one of perpetual fury, and with some alarm I noted the mighty thews displayed below the garment around his middle.

Additionally, he had a torso of monstrous girth, not to mention muscles in his arms the size of fists. These thews seemed to quiver and twitch continually, as if the fellow were

28

in a constant state of truculent tension. He never stopped muttering and growling.

Some sort of talisman dangled from a thong at his waist. I studied it until I realized—with horror!—that it was a dried and shrunken head. Why had this desperate looking and obviously quarrelsome individual chosen my bench? Plainly, the gods had once more withdrawn their favor.

He made himself more comfortable. His broadsword gigged me so sharply that I nearly fell off the bench. He whipped his head around.

"Did you say something, beer-belly?"

"Why, no, no!" I replied in haste, all the while attempting to keep myself from tumbling to the pavement. "Ah—you're a stranger in Atlantis, am I correct?"

His hand lunged for his sword hilt. "What makes you say that?"

"Only your costume!"

"You don't like it?"

"I think it's quite—manly! None of the silly ornamentation of our town fops, no, indeed."

In truth, I didn't know what to say next. With very little provocation, the fellow would wield his blade and ram me through the guts; there was no doubting that he was in that sort of mood. Therefore, I took pains to placate him.

"Indeed, sir, from your apparel, I'd say you've come to the Island Kingdom from a goodly distance. You're a barbarian! From the far north, right?"

"Where else?" was his reply, as he fingered his skin garments.

"Come down to fair Atlantis for a little holiday, is that so?"

"Holiday!" he shrieked, causing heads to turn everywhere. I again thought he meant to spit at me. He spat on the stones instead. "Do you think I wanted to wind up in this misbegotten, god-cursed, devil-plagued place? Not a bit of it! I arrived here only through the most accursed twistings of fate, with nothing save my trusty blade, a pouch of coins"—once more he fixed me with that intemperate stare—"and an intense dislike for everyone I've met so far. Including you."

Just then, I noticed a few scraps of dried seaweed clinging to the hair of his cloak. I indicated them and said:

"You were shipwrecked, perchance?"

"That's putting it mildly! I was a victim of a storm of monstrous proportions. One in which the lightnings flashed ell-bright and the thunder roared like the clap of the gates of doom."

He certainly had a florid way of speaking, but I had no intention of criticizing his rhetoric aloud. After my initial fear began to mitigate—he had sat beside me nearly five minutes, and I was still alive!—I found myself piqued by his churlish manners. Setting aside my notion to simply retreat and let him have the bench all to himself, I began to look on his truculence as something of a challenge.

"My name is Hoptor, sir. I am a lifelong resident of the Island Kingdom. Though I wish you wouldn't mention my name aloud, as I'm currently in some difficulty with the powers that be."

"Ho-ho!" he roared. "A jailbird, is it? A rogue? That's the kind I like!" To display his pleasure, he slapped my back so hard that I did fall off the bench.

When I regained my seat, he seized my hand in a grip that nearly shattered many small bones. "My name is Conax," he said. "In full, Conax the Chimerical. And I've changed my opinion of you. I'm pleased to meet a fellow who has something in his guts other than oatmeal. We're going to be friends, Hopt—"

"Ssh!"

He blinked so many times that I realized with dismay that not only was he of a quick temper, he was none too bright as well. An unhappy combination!

"Oh yes," he said in a vague way, "I forgot."

"And now," cried the auctioneer, "a true vision of feminine charm, radiant in all her tempting pulchritude—ladies and gents, a nice hand for our next offering, the Widow Phlebus! Who'll start the bid at forty zebs?"

Knock-kneed and toothless, poor Widow Phlebus cowered when a man sprang up to cry, "You'll have to pay us to buy that old cow!"

Suddenly my companion likewise jumped to his feet. He whipped his broadsword high over his head and flourished it wildly, shouting, "By Crok, when are we going to see some attractive flesh for a change? If you don't show us something besides grandmothers, auctioneer, I'll come up there and chop off your privates!"

"But, sir—"

"Be quiet! I came here to buy a companion for my loneliness, not a feminine horror sprung from a nightmare!"

About to retort further, the auctioneer took note of Conax's immense stature and quivering thews, then replied that, shortly, he would present an item the gentleman would perhaps find more suitable.

30

"By Crok, you'd better, or you'll roast in the thrice-damned guts of hell's deepest, darkest, most demonic pits!"

So saying, Conax sat down. He was highly flushed.

"So—ah—you're lonesome?" I inquired in my most affable way.

"You don't know the half of it," he answered.

"How long did you say you've been in Atlantis?"

"A fortnight. It seems like centuries."

"And you come from the far north?"

"That's right. I sailed out in command of my goodly band of reavers, our dragon-sail craft bound to plunder the shipping lanes. However, that storm I mentioned caught us by surprise. Our stout vessel foundered, then broke apart. In the midst of the screaming, squalling, storm-lashed holocaust of hell—" There he went again with his heroic phraseology. But prudence prevailed; I merely nodded in an attentive way.

Fingering the hilt of his mighty sword, he went on: "—In the midst of that wailing, thundering, thrice-cursed maelstrom, we sighted the monster."

"Monster?" I replied, starting visibly.

"Indescribably phantasmagoric! A creature from time forgot! A sea-swimming dragon of the most baleful appearance. It loomed amidst the crashing waves and fixed us with its damned glowing eye. Had I been near enough to pierce it with my stout broadsword, it would have, I am certain, gushed pustulant ichor from hell!"

"That's very interesting. But are you sure this monster wasn't some figment of your imagination?"

He whipped up the sword so that its point distressed my belly. "If you're questioning my veracity, Crok knows that I'll send you shrieking to the nether fires!"

"Oh, no, I believe you, I believe you," I said, wiggling away as fast as possible. "By the way, who is this Crok you're constantly invoking?"

"The all-powerful god of the wild, wasted, northern lands," said Conax, rolling his eyes skyward in a devout manner.

"You and your—ah—reavers were cast adrift following the shipwreck?"

"Save for myself, all hands were lost. I managed to cling to a bit of wreckage, endure the chaos of the cosmos raining down upon me, and was subsequently washed up on your unfriendly shore. Thus you find me, abandoned and alone. I have, however, inscribed a message, inserted it in a winegourd, and thrown it into the sea. Eventually it will reach my homeland, whereupon my stout host will jump on the first available

31

dragon-sail ship and come to fetch me." With a grisly smile he added, "When they get here, they just may show you mincing Atlanteans a thing or two."

Blanching, I asked, "What do you mean?"

"Very likely they'll sack, loot, rape, burn, and murder. They're that sort. Being their leader, so am I."

"Uh—can you tell me what happened to the sea-dragon?"

"Disappeared! Right at the height of the storm, too. Doubtless it feared to face the sword of Conax the Chimerical." His glee as he stroked the blade made me quake.

Next he informed me, "This is the very iron which has dispatched devils, demons, imps, wizards, warlocks, one or two witches, and monsters without numbering. As leader of my barbaric band, I've roved o'er the known Earth, seen sights to dazzle the mind and petrify the faint of heart. By the way, you Atlanteans seem very proud of this miserable sea-prisoned isle. But as one who has traveled widely, I must inform you that it can't hold a candle to Lemuria."

Nothing so fired the ire of we citizens of the Island Kingdom as invidious comparisons with that sink of depravity half around the world. However, I continued to humor Conax by maintaining a manful silence.

With a faint crawl of horrific dread on my scalp, I did wonder at his tale of a sea-dragon. If he were not lying, then dark forces might indeed be gathering round our happy homeland. The prophecies of Babylos might come true after all.

"—Attention, please, especially you gentlemen of lusty appetites! Here is the prime offering of the morning mart. Her sportive nature proved too vigorous for her owner, one of the foremost citizens of fair Atlantis. Thus, with great reluctance, he offers her upon the block, to bring joy to another."

Here and there in the crowd, hoots and sneers testified that the auctioneer's sham was recognized for what it was. I also caught a remark concerning Captain Num's jealousy. On the block, dear Aphrodisia stood in manacles, looking somehow more naked by the morning's light than she had last evening.

Head up, red hair tossing in the breeze, she appeared both defiant and a bit pathetic. She scanned the faces below, hoping for succor.

I sat forward on my portion of the bench. The crucial moment had arrived.

Of course I longed to reveal my presence by flinging aside my cowl. But I felt sure that as soon as I began bidding,

Aphrodisia would recognize me. And she would know that her troubles were over.

Mine, however, were just beginning.

"That's more like it!" Conax announced. "Just what a shipwrecked barbarian needs to warm the long nights and assuage his loneliness." So saying, he produced a large purse of coins.

"Oh, no, take my advice," I exclaimed, trying to conceal my concern. "I know that baggage. She has a tongue like an asp."

"And the body of a goddess! I'll do the talking for both of us."

"I can't begin the bidding at anything less than seventy zebs," the auctioneer stated.

Conax leaped to his feet and flourished his sword. "That's what I bid!"

The auctioneer paled. "It's only necessary, sir, to raise your hand. Brandishing weapons is not required."

"All right, but I've bought her, haven't I?"

"No, sir, not yet," returned the auctioneer, visibly intimidated by the spectacle of the huge barbarian quivering and twitching over every square inch of his exposed and bulging thews.

"I doubt anyone will bid against me," he said, sitting down and holding his sword in a distinctly menacing way.

At that point, of course, I could have kept my peace. I could have retired from all further controversy. But I had vowed to regain Aphrodisia for my vineyard, and, in truth, I did not care for the burly rascal's badgering ways. Screwing up my nerve, I raised my hand.

The auctioneer cried, "Seventy-five zebs from the gentleman in the cloak."

"What?" Conax thundered. "Bidding against me?"

"Well, I get as lonely as the next."

A fat lot of good that did to damp the flaming wrath of his blue eyes! Aphrodisia recognized me then, I believe. She clapped her hands and uttered a small squeal of joy.

I fully expected Conax to gut me on the spot. Instead, he clenched his jaw and waved his fist.

"I have eighty zebs!" was the auctioneer's response.

Up went my hand, then down, then up. The auctioneer sounded almost delirious as he exclaimed, "One hundred! Do I hear a hundred and ten?"

"Two hundred, you dog!" howled Conax.

The auctioneer cracked his whip. "I hear two hundred—"

Suddenly Aphrodisia rushed to whisper in his ear. His eyes narrowed. She had evidently communicated the fact that she only wished to be sold to me, the dear girl! Certainly, the auctioneer would favor me, a citizen, above the ill-mannered outlander with his posturing air of bravado.

Almost immediately, this was proved so, as the auctioneer proclaimed, "No, I only hear one hundred."

"You hear two hundred!" Conax thundered, striking his blade on the bench. As the sparks shot off and the ringing died, he glowered hideously at the auctioneer. "You also hear the knell of your own funeral, if you ignore my bid again."

"I—I—I hear two hundred."

"Three hundred!" I shouted.

"Four hundred!" Conax yelled.

"Five hundred!"

I was mad! I was delirious with the excitement of the moment! Aphrodisia, the little minx, was enjoying herself immensely. In a trice, the bid was raised by Conax to the positively calamitous figure of one thousand zebs, at which time I rose from the bench.

The crowd groaned. The auctioneer's face fell. Aphrodisia looked as though she had been betrayed into the grasp of the fiend himself.

"Giving up, eh?" Conax grinned.

"Merely answering nature's call," I said, promising him I would be back.

The auctioneer took my cue, pretending to find something amiss with Aphrodisia's chains. Thus I had time to hurry to the door of the building where the mart manager lounged, beaming over the handsome sums being bandied in the air.

I seized his arm and tugged him inside. "You've got to help me! Divert that rascal's attention or we'll be bidding till the sun goes down."

"Splendid idea! We might set a record. Ten thousand zebs, do you think?"

"You'd better think twice before you let your greed run away with you, my friend. If I were to send a message to certain official quarters—and if the bearer of the message were to mention my name, thereby validating the source of the information—there'd be quite a hue and cry. Also an official investigation of the way in which you come by some of the youngsters you bargain away on that block. Would you care to have it known that your gangs linger outside the day schools, luring innocent tots into alleys with promises of

34

sweetmeats? Would you care to have a general broadcast of the way in which those precious little ones are stripped of identification, thrust into mealsacks, and hustled to your cells, there to await—?"

"Enough!" he quavered. "You've made me see the error of my ways, Hoptor. What price profit if a man loses his slaver's license?"

"That's more like it," I said, and told him what he must do.

Returning to my seat, I discovered Conax the Chimerical counting his coins. He had spread them on the bench, thus depriving me of any room whatsoever. His belligerent stare invited me to question his behavior at my peril. Naturally, I did not.

"All right, let's get on with it, you lewd looking bag of bones," Conax called to the auctioneer.

A certain increased tension now gripped the entire mart, all assembled craning around to watch the financial duel. Without doubt, I had been recognized by more than a few; sympathy was entirely on my side.

Aphrodisia, however, appeared to be deeply worried about the outcome. Hastily, if reluctantly, I calculated the limits of my credit. Then I announced a bid of one thousand, two hundred zebs.

In a rage, Conax screamed, "One thousand, three hundred."

"Four!"

"Five!"

Dare I leap to two thousand in order to save the day? What was detaining the idiot manager? In a feeble voice, the auctioneer began, "Do I hear—?"

"I'll teach you to try to snatch my purse, you little imp!"

All heads, including that of Conax, turned. The manager was boxing the ears of one of his grimy office boys. I alone ignored the charade, concentrating my attention upon the clock. I raised my fist, then frantically signaled for the end of bidding.

The auctioneer cracked his whip twice and cried, "One thousand, six hundred zebs! Sold to the gentleman in the cloak."

"What?" The howl of Conax was as the roar of the thunderstorm. "What? Gulled? Tricked? Bilked? You can't do this to a king of Chimeria!"

And before I could so much as move one single step, he lifted the bench with writhing thews and threw it at my head.

I ducked, but the unlucky fellow behind me did not. Gasp-

35

ing, he collapsed. Aphrodisia's squeal of joy changed to a wail of fright.

"Here, let's have none of that!" exclaimed the auctioneer, with several smart cracks of the whip. But it was too late. Conax the Chimerical was brandishing his broadsword and bellowing at the top of his lungs:

"Death and damnation! I'll take you all to hell's dark deeps, Crok if I won't!"

So saying, he charged at me with sword bared, making me rue my decision to defy the whims of a mighty barbarian. Once again, Aphrodisia had certainly landed me in a pretty mess!

✳ Four ✳

I had only a heartbeat's time in which to extricate myself from the unhappy predicament symbolized by Conax's fearsome weapon darting—flashing!—in the direction of my stomach. The barbarian's face wrenched into what he presumed was a smile of triumph. Promptly, I shifted the center of my weight, and directed my entire person downward.

My rump smacked the stones. My legs flew out in front of me—in essence, I had sat down—and the wicked blade slashed through the area in which my waistline had been located but a moment before.

King Conax—if indeed he was the ruler he pretended to be!—shrieked vengefully, discovering his equilibrium affected by the massive thrust. Too late to brake his charge, he followed his sword, which contacted the shanks of a fishmonger of my acquaintance.

The latter, an old gaffer, had been attempting to flee the sudden melee, and was caught unexpectedly by Conax's shaft. The old fellow squealed, leaped, thereby scattering the contents of a basket of odorous smelts upon which he'd been snacking.

"Oh, you cut me, you cut me!" cried he, waving his bloodied robe with one hand while collecting smelts to hurl with the other. In truth, Conax had struck low, a mere flesh wound. But you might have thought the barbarian had sent the old man to his ancestors, so wrathfully did the fishmonger hurl fish.

Conax slipped on a mess of fish. He collapsed on hands and knees. He was prevented from arising by blows from nearby friends of the smelt-nibbler. I, for one, did not fare much better.

I received a stiff box on the ears. Someone yelled, "Hoptor, you coward, that was a dastardly maneuver!"

"Are you willing to let a grandfather fight your battles?" exclaimed another, kicking me smartly in the ribs.

With noise and confusion mounting everywhere, I felt that it was not a prudent moment to enter into a discussion of my strategies. The backward citizens could not appreciate that my sitting down was merely the triumph of a sharp mind and responsive body over brute force.

Cowardice, indeed!

"By Crok, where is he? Somebody point me toward that mountain of flab—!"

So saying, Conax batted aside assorted fish and personal items—beads, pebbles, even a few zebs—flung at him by the irate citizenry. A quick glance informed me that his position made it impossible for him to locate me at once. He was turned the other way, and still suffering many indignities. That gave me a chance to roll over. Stomach downward, I began to scuttle away in the manner of an ocean crab.

Kicked, gouged, bumped, I nevertheless managed to put a fair distance between myself and the quivering-thewed warrior, while all around, men and women rushed every which way, clamoring:

"Murther, murther!!" (That was the fishmonger. His outcries certainly didn't help restore order; I marveled at the lack of bravery of certain members of our populace.)

"Let's flee, it's a riot!"

"Too late! Here come the soldiers!"

These remarks reached my ears through a forest of churning legs. Intemperate slave-buyers were picking up benches and hurling them. Neighbor was assaulting neighbor without pretext or warning. Oaths grew more pungent, not to say blasphemous, and in the hurly-burly, everyone was attempting to escape at one time.

I ventured to rise into a semi-crouch, searching for my purchase of the morning. All at once I came face to face with a militaristic plug-ugly, one of a platoon no doubt hastily summoned when the fracas broke out. The whole mart remained in a turmoil, and of a sudden I heard the word "arrest" being bandied about.

I do not rightly know how many of Pytho's minions thronged into the slave mart on short notice. But it seemed to be regiments. The plug-ugly previously noted rushed me and attempted to wrap a rope around my chest.

"No, no, release me! I'm only passing through! I'm a messenger on my way to—"

He stoppered my protests with a blow of his fist.

It is not true, as was later charged, that I bit him on the wrist in sheer panic. There was no panic; I knew precisely what I was doing.

But I didn't manage to escape.

Of that confused and horrendous confrontation, I mercifully remember little more, for what happened next was humiliating in the extreme. I, lifelong resident of the Island Kingdom, was arrested without a warrant and hustled off. Of course, quite a few others were in like position, as I discovered when my senses unfogged.

A straggling procession of two or three dozen Atlanteans limped along in a direction all too familiar. Soldiers flanked the line of prisoners. It seemed that an unusually large number guarded me, fore, aft, and to either side. I soon learned why.

The various citizens swept into the official net gestured rudely—not to say ferociously—whenever my eye chanced to meet theirs.

Swiveling my head, I espied Aphrodisia behind me. She lifted her nose and gazed elsewhere.

Further back, restrained by thick cords, the ends of which were held by fully a dozen men, Conax saw me staring. He began to lunge like a wild beast after a meal. The soldier fought to hold him, for he seemed ready to burst his bond by sheer expansion and contraction of his thews.

In short, I had the distinct impression that virtually all of those who hadn't escaped held me personally responsible for their arrest. Of weak moral fiber, they obviously hadn't the stomach for accusing the true perpetrator—Conax. So the guilt became mine. I kept my head down and studied my toes, wondering how I could extricate myself from this predicament.

As I feared, our route led directly to a grim structure near the palace. We were thrust into a queue on the main floor, inspected by a soldier with tablet and stylus, and forced to make our marks. Then we were led downward at least two flights, to the foul, airless confines of the dungeons.

As we passed along the damp passage, other prisoners—dregs of our Island society!—idled between the bars and exchanged comments at our expense:

"Say, isn't that old Hoptor? Did your grapes run away and report you to the authorities?"

"Notice that redhead. Oh, sergeant! What about putting her in my cell? I get chilly at night."

"Who's the muscle man wearing all those hides? Some carnival entertainer?"

This last provoked Conax to a maniacal howl. Before the soldiers could react, he flashed his hands through the bars and half throttled the unfortunate who had failed to recognize his kingly demeanor.

I grew more dismayed every moment, for I knew that I might be in for some unpleasantness when I was abandoned in one of the cells with my fellow captives. And so it came to pass, when we were herded into a large barred enclosure.

Instantly I found myself ringed by antagonists. They backed me slowly into an offal-strewn corner. I raised my hands.

"One moment, friends! If you'll give me leave to explain—"

"You got us into this, you pandering rogue!" exclaimed a matron whose eye makeup had been ludicrously smeared. The others growled assent to her charge.

I looked in vain at Aphrodisia. With arms crossed over her bosoms—it was fiendish cold in those dripping cellars!—she was content to remain at the back of the pack, smugly enjoying my discomfort.

"Let me through!" boomed a voice. "I'll tally up his accounts!"

But Conax was thrust back by the others.

"It's just as much your fault, you ill-bred foreigner. Leave this to us!"

Conax's thews vibrated vigorously. "What, balk me? Stand aside, you crawling cravens—!"

This outburst was jeered, and he was punched roundly by the crowd, there being safety in numbers. In a moment, he subsided. He withdrew to sulk and shoot menacing glances in my direction. I caught his remark to the effect that the citizens would chant a different anthem when his looting, raping, murdering reavers arrived to rescue him.

Growling once more, the crowd shuffled forward in my direction. But having frowned for a lengthy period, the gods saw fit to change their mood.

A spear rattled on the bars. Metal clanged metal. A burly soldier announced:

"Here's lunch, you dogs."

The reeking swillpot poured its unwholesome fumes over

the entire cell, causing many gasps. The matron fainted upon the befouled straw.

Someone sampled the brew, and spat it out. Someone else suggested I be placed headfirst in the pot.

"Wait, wait!" I protested. "If you'll only give me leave to speak to the officer in charge, perhaps I can remedy our plight. You forget that Hoptor the Vintner is not without friends in Atlantis."

"All right," was the decision. "You have one minute. Then it's into the pot with you."

"Sergeant? Sergeant, in heaven's name——!" I rattled the bars noisily. When that scowling worthy presented himself, I leaned forward and whispered, "It's urgent that you take a message to the commander of the prison. Good Menos is still in charge, isn't he?"

"He is. But he's out to lunch."

"The moment he returns, inform him that Hoptor the Vintner wishes to speak to him. Be sure to mention my name."

"Why should I?"

"Because if you don't, he's liable to demote you. There is a certain matter of two female teachers of mathematics— and a pickle-shaped birthmark—" Switching tactics, I gestured grandly. "But see here! I'll not bandy with lesser fry."

"Fancy this," exclaimed the soldier. "Being ordered about by a fat-shanked jailbird. Any other instructions for me, porky?"

All my years of assiduously cultivating citizens of every stamp, from one end of fair Atlantis to the other, came to my assistance once more, in the form of a prisoner down the hall who chimed in:

"If that's truly Hoptor, friend, you had better convey the message. The Vintner has influence in unusual quarters."

The sergeant reflected upon this. Without answering yea or nay, he took himself away up the slimy corridor. Putting on a good front, I turned to my fellow-prisoners.

"You'll see, we'll get results—and soon!"

We certainly did—though not as I anticipated!

About an hour later, soldiers invaded the cell. Most of the citizens were hustled out, to their surprise and glee. Only Conax, Aphrodisia, and I were restrained behind a barricade of spears.

"What's this new indignity?" I cried. "They're being let go and we're not?"

"They're to be fined for disturbing the peace," replied the sergeant whom I had sent on the mission.

"Did you not carry word to Menos?"

"I did, and it's on his orders that you three are being detained. However, he did instruct us to take you to the roof and permit you to exercise." He seized me by the cowl of my cloak. "Menos will speak to you there, you—influence-peddler!"

"Good-bye, Hoptor, and many thanks!" chorused the citizens, trooping off up the stairs to freedom.

Aphrodisia, Conax and I were led up another stairway. The barbarian had fallen into a sullen silence, nibbling his lips and glowering from under his brows. As we were hustled along, I contrived to place myself next to Aphrodisia.

"Don't worry, dear," I whispered. "I'm sure my friendship with Menos will get us out."

She tossed her red curls and said to Conax, "Would you be so good as to inform this person that, even though he purchased me, I am not speaking to him?"

"Tell him yourself, you devil's daughter," Conax returned, in a pet.

Severely short of breath from climbing several flights, I emerged into an unnatural darkness. The spacious roof of the drab old building was being lashed by a stiff wind. And instead of clear blue heavens above, my eyes beheld a sky of fast-sailing gray clouds. Indeed, it looked as if night was nigh. Beyond the rooftops and the seawall, the mighty ocean was a frenzy of foam.

Perhaps three dozen souls who had fallen victim to Atlantean justice were tottering back and forth on the roof, watched by Pytho's armored bullies. Yonder at the parapet, I spied a familiar figure—seedy old Babylos. Instead of exercising, he stood with head thrown back, regarding the clouds with mad concentration.

Conax and Aphrodisia moved off, the latter shivering because of her near-nudity. This aroused lascivious stares and remarks from prisoners and guards, you may be sure.

There was a sudden tug at my sleeve. I turned to confront emaciated, one-eyed Menos.

"I received your message, Hoptor."

"Then I trust you will shortly rectify the mistake."

He scratched a white eyebrow and sucked a yellow tooth. "Uh—mistake?"

"Definitely. Why weren't we freed with the rest?"

"Because, old friend, I have orders to the contrary."

"What?" I exclaimed, feigning horror. "Can my ears be hearing aright? Is this the same Menos who, through my in-

41

ervention, was relieved of the burden of disproving not one but two separate charges of paternity levied by those lewd lady mathematics teachers? Am I listening to the same keeper of the royal jails who was set free from the haunting memory of a birthmark shaped like a pickle?"

"Must you keep mentioning that wench's particular—?"

"I certainly must, until friendship repays friendship!"

Leaning close—and giving me a whiff of his leek-perfumed breath, I don't mind saying!—he confided, "Hoptor, I would swing the prison doors open if I could. I am ever in your debt—just like a majority of the population."

"Those curs in the dungeon had rather short memories. They would have mauled me for starting the melee at the mart. In truth, that blustering son of the steppes caused the entire affair."

"You refer to that one over there, the brute who calls himself King Conax?"

"Who else?"

"A desperate sort, I'm advised."

"Down in the dungeon," I went on, "I distinctly glimpsed at least three people for whom I've done favors. Did they remember? Did they acknowledge it? Did they even know me? They did not—except as objects of their wrath! Now," I added, with as much significance as I could muster, "it seems that even older, truer friends suffer the same convenient lapse of memory."

"There is nothing I can do, Hoptor!"

"Why not?"

"Because Captain Num himself inspected the roster of prisoners. And personally made a mark beside your name—"

"That vengeful pretty-boy!" I cried, flailing my fists at heaven.

"—not to mention the name of your—ah—vintage. Num insisted that she is General Pytho's property."

"Oh? I figured he would want to get rid of her. Well, no doubt he weighed the choices, and found toadying to Pytho more advantageous than disposing of a romantic rival."

"The captain also marked the name of Conax, who has been under observation ever since he arrived in fair Atlantis. Conax has been identified as a troublemaker and undesirable. For one thing, he's started a whole string of tavern fights. Thus, for various reasons, I have strict orders to hold all three of you, until—"

He trailed off in somewhat ominous fashion, casting his eyes to the cloud-streaming heavens.

42

"In the name of the gods, don't leave me dangling, Menos! We are to be held until what happens?"

"I don't think you'll be long in discovering that, Hoptor. I am informed that this very afternoon—"

Again the melodramatic pause, which only served to set my skin to crawling. Thereupon he grew even more confidential.

"I would repay your past help tenfold. But take my word— the situation forbids it."

I drew myself up wrathfully. "In other words, as a venal bureaucrat, your position in the system means more to you than debts of honor?"

"Actually, it's not my position that concerns me, it's my head."

"But at very least, you can tell me what is supposed to happen this aft—"

"Look, look! Calamity and corruption have at last reaped their harvest!"

This strident, not to say startling, cry electrified the entire rooftop, causing all heads to swivel in the direction in which mad Babylos was pointing.

His palsied finger indicated the high heavens, across which, unless my eyes confounded me, fully a dozen disc-shaped apparitions flashed at fantastical speed.

The shapes radiated a strange, brilliant light. In addition, they maintained a uniform distance one from another. Without warning, all turned left—or southward—simultaneously.

Soldiers began falling to their knees. Aphrodisia gripped the parapet. Even Conax appeared dumbfounded.

"There are the signs!" Babylos shrieked, the very figure of a prophet, his long white beard flapping in the wind. "Those are the manifestations I have seen in the heavens before! There is my proof that the gods are displeased!"

"Have we all gone crazy?" Menos said. "I see them too."

"You're not the only one," I told him, rushing over to the old soothsayer. "Babylos, I thought your talk of heavenly discs was mere prattling. Forgive me, can you?"

"Vindicated!" he crowed, beating his fists on the parapet gleefully. "Perhaps now the people will heed my words— recognize that the imperial line has rotted—O Geriasticus, thy hour approaches! O Voluptua, thy depravities bring forth divine wrath! Doom gathers round fair Atlantis—doom, doom—!"

And, kicking and thrashing, he fell to the roof There he writhed in a lively fashion. But, it must be admitted, he seemed unusually happy the while!

As for me, my flesh stirred—not to say crept!—at the unnatural sight of those eerie lights veering again. Traveling with incredible swiftness, they came streaking back across the heavens. In a trice they were directly overhead.

Aphrodisia flung herself into my arms. "Protect me, Hoptor, I'm terrified!"

"I—I—I thought you weren't speaking to me."

"That was before those lights appeared. Is it the end of the world?"

"Certainly not," I replied, though with little conviction. "There must be some natural explanation—"

"Doom, doom, that's the explanation!" Babylos wailed, rolling about in animated fashion. Two trembling soldiers whacked him with spear-butts, silencing his outcries temporarily.

"Had I my broadsword," Conax announced, "I would fly at those phantasmagorical lanterns and slay them, slay in red fury, slay—!" And he began to hop and caper, making passes with an imaginary blade, performing what I supposed must be a ritual dance of his native country. Aphrodisia snuffled and snuggled closer.

"At least those dreadful lights take his mind off you."

"Oh? I thought you wanted me dispatched to the nether regions."

"I keep thinking I should want that! But I just haven't the heart to see it happen, no matter how ill you treat me. Love is unpredictable, isn't it, Hoptor? And bittersweet, now that we obviously have little time left to enjoy it. Do you suppose there's a prison chaplain who could—?"

"And with my killing iron, I'd skewer you, too, you thrice-branded barrel of bilge!" Conax informed me, as if to make certain I realized he still bore a grudge. "I'd do it with my own mighty hands, this instant—but that's letting you off too easily!"

Just then, another party of soldiers appeared. They demanded to know what all the fuss was about.

I swung and discovered that, in a twinkling, the discs of light had vanished to the eastward.

Menos rushed up and whispered:

"I'm afraid the rope's run out, Hoptor. Those men have orders to bring you, your wench, the barbarian, and that traitor Babylos before none other than Geriasticus X himself."

"For vindication!" I announced, mainly for Aphrodisia's benefit. Privately, I was concerned that the mass judgment might have an entirely different outcome!

✳ Five ✳

Brazen horns tootled. Massed tympani bumped and thumped in an ostentatious way. Two mighty metal doors, each displaying the bossed sigil of the Geriastic kings, began to swing inward.

The doors squeaked. The sycophants of the imperial palace were too caught up in their pell-mell pursuit of pleasure to handle menial housekeeping chores!

From the screened music gallery, some court functionary cried out:

"Abase thyselves! Abase thyselves all before the Light of the Middle Sea—His Exaltedness—Geriasticus X!"

Conax, Aphrodisia, Babylos, and your servant stood shoulder to shoulder in the yawning doorway. Each performed the abasement with varying degrees of alacrity, I being the first to fall on my knees and knock my forehead on the cracked stones. Lest you think this mere cowardice, inspired by the presence of quite a few heavily armed soldiers directly behind us, I must report the truth of the matter. I merely wished to survey the throne room from a safe vantage point.

Thus, with my nose flat to the floor, I peered through my eyebrows—no mean feat!—and tried to ascertain who was present, in order that I might estimate who would be favorable to our cause, and who not.

One glance and my spirits sank. I had a few acquaintances in the chamber, but no one I could truly call a friend.

Aphrodisia abased herself immediately after I did. But Babylos was slow. He received a thwack in the pate from a soldier.

"You heard him—abase!"

Babylos did, albeit muttering the while.

I might have counted on the Chimerical one to show foolish resistance.

"A king of the north country abases himself before no one. By Crok, I refuse to—oww!"

Several spear-butts, lavishly applied to his head, sent the

contentious fellow to his knees. There, he proceeded to bark, paw the air, and make other threatening noises. The soldiers stayed out of his way.

In truth, I was beginning to feel a sort of unbidden sympathy for the big lout. The instincts of his pulsing thews were forever being checked by this or that authoritarian decree. Perhaps on the treeless steppes from which he hailed, merely biting or maiming anyone who disagreed would serve to remove the obstacle. But here in fair Atlantis, other, more artful means of opposition were called for. And he understood them not.

At a command of the hidden voice, we began to crawl forward into the throne room. If you have ever planned a strategy while scraping your forehead over some ill-fitting stones, you know the plight of Hoptor the Vintner just then!

Around the vast hall, a few courtiers lolled on couches, divans, and cushions. For the most part, they seemed intoxicated out of their wits by the wine which rouged page boys dispensed at a snap of a ringed finger. Among the nobles I did recognize several who had ordered vintages from me. But even if the fellows were sober, I knew they'd never acknowledge doing business. Not in the presence of the depraved coterie around the throne!

Highest of all in his carven chair was the wearer of the purple, Geriasticus X. He was ninety if he was an hour.

An old skin-and-bones with a pathetic wisp of chin-beard, Geriasticus X had long ago lost his natural teeth. He had been fitted with a set of ivory replacements—flawless, I might note! —which lent his face a touch of grotesque glee. Several barebosomed courtesans clustered near his footstool, attempting to lave his feet in bowls of steaming, flower-scented water. Due to his palsy, the carpets, not to mention the courtesans, were constantly being splashed.

Below him on the tiered dais, I shuddered to see my nemesis, General Pytho. Sans armor, he swilled wine and grinned ghoulishly.

At Pytho's feet lounged Captain Num, seemingly content to stare into space and have his curled locks toyed with. Perhaps old Babylos had indeed rung the gong when he ranted of courtly depravity!

To my consternation, the queen, Lady Voluptua, was nowhere present. Off amusing herself with a member of her legion of lovers, no doubt! Her absence immediately aborted one of my survival schemes.

Not that it would have been guaranteed to succeed; a side

long glance showed me Conax still crawling along muttering oaths, as if the spear-blows had affected his mind. Hardly a prepossessing specimen!

When we reached the foot of the dais, Geriasticus X raised a ringed hand. Due to his advanced years, the act required several minutes to complete.

When he addressed us, he took an intolerable time just uttering a single word; for the sake of clarity and swiftness of narrative, I shall editorially abridge his gasps, groans, and other vocal interpolations.

"All may rise and face Our Exaltedness. What, pray, are the charges?"

A functionary carrying several rolled scrolls rushed to the dais and knocked his head. I recognized Writtus, of the legal profession. Shamelessly flattering the old king in the hope of being appointed a Judge, you may be sure!

Writtus had a wife and many children. But he frequently availed himself of my vintages, at hired rooms on Rotten Row. Of course he didn't know me from an incense burner this afternoon!

"There are separate and individual charges against each, Your Exaltedness," Writtus said. He proffered an unrolled scroll, which Geriasticus pretended to be able to read.

"We desire to spare ourselves the burden of dealing with such lowly offenders," said the king, again with clicks of his ivory mouth-ware, and gasps far too numerous to indicate. "We only received these prisoners at the request of our military commander. Our esteemed General Pytho has informed us that they're all malcontents. He charges that, in their various ways, they have disturbed the order and tranquility of fair Atlantis!"

Pytho's pug face was wreathed in pleasure. His fine hand in arranging this charade was certainly not hidden!

Geriasticus remained pettish about the whole affair, though. He didn't care for using what remained of his mind to make judicial pronouncements. It was much easier to simply lie about and have one's toes laved with scented water!

"Therefore, learned Writtus," the king said, "you may inform us of the offenses—but briefly!"

Strutting self-consciously, the lawyer said, "First we have the matter of treasonous speech, uttered on several occasions by yonder Babylos."

"Babylos, Babylos—" The king rolled his eyes and squinted. "Pray inform us—which one is he?" He seemed to be studying Aphrodisia's thighs.

47

"On the left, Your Exaltedness."

"Oh yes, indeed," said Geriasticus X, swiveling his head toward Conax.

"No, no," exclaimed Writtus, "the left!"

General Pytho jumped to his feet, hurling his winecup away. "Are you inferring that His Exaltedness is not familiar with the separateness of right and left, you hair-splitting scum?"

Writtus blanched, while Num tittered behind manicured nails. General Pytho's behavior was both obvious and reprehensible. He would literally stop at nothing to advance himself; and his tactics included humiliation of anyone who might gain even a moment's favor with the monarch.

To his credit, Writtus made a bold defense.

"I meant, naturally, the left of His Exaltedness, rather than the left of the line of prisoners as viewed from their own vantage point. Forgive my opaque phraseology, Exaltedness!" he added, falling on his knees and knocking his head several times.

"Don't let it happen again," the king remarked, causing Pytho to fall back in his chair, smirking.

At length, Geriasticus X focused upon Babylos. The old scholar kept his chin high, his glance unflinching. Not my style, certainly! But if he wished to cast his life away in an empty gesture, that was his affair.

"Babylos," mused the king. "A name once highly honored in our Island Kingdom—"

"But now he spews out all manner of poison against the throne," Pytho barked. "Unfounded claims—mad accusations—"

"That's what comes of too much reading," was the king's considered opinion.

"Then take my head for it!" said Babylos. "I will go to my death affirming that I have seen signs!"

"What?" Geriasticus X cried. "You not only speak against us, but post inflammatory circulars?"

"Signs in the heavens! This very afternoon, for example. From the prison roof, I sighted shining lights—glowing discs flying overhead at great speed. Surely an indication of the mounting displeasure of the gods!"

"What twaddle is this of lights?" Pytho thundered, on his feet again. "Were any of you soldiers at the prison when this alleged sighting took place?"

"Yes, General," chorused the phalanx behind us.

48

"And did any of you lay eyes on these so-called heavenly gleams?"

"No, General," they shouted, to a man.

"You see, Your Exaltedness? Revolutionary lies!"

I observed Conax glowering in astonishment just then. Plainly, he was about to blurt that he had seen the illuminated portents. But he didn't, though his mouth remained open. At last, something had shocked him to silence! Namely, a sample of royal card-stacking!

I swallowed a hen's egg in my throat, and wiped my palms upon my cloak. My mind still raced, seeking a way to offset the dire direction the interview was taking. Babylos, however, would not be stopped.

"Let me rot in prison forever——!" Why was he constantly inviting these harmful consequences? "But I will not recant. Doom is ordained for fair Atlantis, unless our government reforms at once!"

"High treason," Geriasticus clacked. "Next case."

While Babylos snorted scornfully, Writtus examined his scroll.

His eye fell upon me. You might have thought I was some loathsome sea-imp!

"A civil matter, Your Exaltedness. Pandering. The guilty party is the portly fellow, Hoptor the Vintner."

"Hoptor, Hoptor," mumbled the king. "One of our more popular citizens, if memory serves."

"Yes, Your Exaltedness, that's true!" I said. "Hoptor the Vintner strives to be a friend to all. Furthermore, he is a vigorous supporter of the throne and all its policies."

Determined to lower the menacing tone of the audience, I rushed on, heedless of Babylos' obvious outrage:

"Yes, never let it be said that Hoptor the Vintner is not in full support of the wise, just, and statesmanlike decrees which emanate from your august personage. In fact, I was remarking to dinner party guests just last night that I knew of no age in the history of Atlantis in which such peace, such prosperity, such enlightened rule has prevailed."

"Is that a fact?" replied the king. "How many guests heard you say that, Hoptor? We are always anxious to discover the extent of our popularity."

On the point of replying—concern for the welfare of my fellow prisoners uppermost in my mind!—I was prevented by an outburst from that scarred schemer, Pytho:

"No guests, Your Exaltedness. There was no dinner party."

"Then did our ears deceive us, General?"

"No, but slop-guts is trying to. There was no dinner party because there couldn't have been. At the dinner hour yesterday, Hoptor the Vintner was accompanying that red-haired baggage to a hired assignation. I personally apprehended him, and I have an objective witness to verify my statement."

He nudged Captain Num, who promptly announced, "Yes, Your Exaltedness, that's one hundred and ten percent right. We caught Hoptor on his way to sell that—*girl*—for a night of lechery. Ooo, it's disgusting!" he concluded, tucking the general's hand against his cheek.

"For shame, Vintner!" Geriasticus said. "Attempting to deceive our royal self!"

"Perhaps I did make an error, Your Exaltedness. The dinner party was the night before last. Fully thirty guests at my villa heard me proclaim my unswerving—"

"Pandering," Geriasticus intoned. "It carries a heavy penalty. Next case."

"The female is his consort in crime," Writtus told him. "Aphrodisia is her name. She has been condemned to a gutter life by Hoptor's unwholesome direction."

Pytho nodded weightily, and at once I smelled more trouble. Pytho said, "This case need not trouble you overlong, Exaltedness. I personally will see to the young lady's moral correction. She has already become my property, in fact. When I am convinced that she has sloughed off the Vintner's depraved influence—an influence no doubt reinforced by drugs, hypnotism, and arcane spells!—I will return her to a useful role in society. I merely wished her summoned to your presence in order that you might endorse my protective custody."

At that Captain Num couldn't conceal a scathing glance at Aphrodisia. She, with blue eyes blazing, sprang to her own defense.

"Protective custody indeed! Your Exaltedness, the general wishes to turn a profit off my predicament. He has taken over my keep in order to sell me in the slave mart and pocket the zebs. Only this morning, I was up on the block, shivering and being subjected to obscene stares—"

"Oh, a tissue of lies, a tissue of lies!" Pytho proclaimed with extravagant gestures.

"It is no such thing!"

Pytho pulled a maudlin face. "Poor helpless child. Obviously still in the Vintner's power. Oh well. A week of my moral instruction and she'll be free of the vapors beclouding her mind."

50

"Hoptor?" Aphrodisia said, wheeling. She was obviously beside herself with fear and unhappiness. "If you care for me, support my story!"

"Well, ah, actually—now that I reconstruct—the head count at my dinner party was fifty at least. Fifty leading citizens, each of whom heard me swear my loyalty and eternal devotion—"

"Oh, you're impossible!" she wailed, stamping her pretty little sandaled foot as tears coursed down both cheeks.

It availed nothing for me to dart glances at her; the misinformed minx believed I was trying to save my own hide. Which proves again how shortsighted and impractical women are. She would continue to offend the court at our peril—and offend it she did, by marching—uninvited—to the foot of the dais.

Sycophants all around the hall gasped in shock. Through her weeping, Aphrodisia exclaimed:

"Perhaps Babylos is right. This Island Kingdom has become a sink of inconvenient illegalities. Honest, common folk have no chance to plead the truth—"

"Have a care!" Writtus warned. "Get back in your place, or you'll be subject to the same penalties as your paramour, the generosity and reformative measures of General Pytho notwithstanding!"

But the unwise child would not leave off.

"Answer me one question, lawyer. If I were married to Hoptor the Vintner—"

Num said, "Ooo, what a repulsive thought!"

Writtus fumed. "What possible connection can the connubial state have with—?"

"You answer me!" she countered, with such fire that Writtus let his scroll roll up with a snap. "If I were married to Hoptor, could I be punished by this tribunal?"

Geriasticus clicked his ivory teeth, saying, "We cannot see where this inquiry is leading, Writtus. But you are permitted to answer the girl's question."

Writtus scowled, then stated:

"Under the statutes of the Island Kingdom, young woman, no more than one member of a family may stand in legal jeopardy at a given time. Therefore, if you were married, you could not be sentenced on the same occasion as your husband. But I am not aware that you are matrimonially linked with this Hoptor—"

"No, I am not. But it's clear I wouldn't be in this fix if I were!"

51

And, stamping back to her place in line, she fixed me with a tearful, accusing stare.

Leave it to a woman to reprimand a man at the most unlikely moment! In typically feminine fashion, Aphrodisia could think of nothing except my failure to honor my various promises of matrimony. She wanted that clearly on the record.

Well, there is simply no accounting for the aberrations of the opposite sex. But is it any wonder that we men cavil at admitting members of her gender to the hardheaded world of commerce and industry?

"Next case, next case!" exclaimed Geriasticus, beginning to look exceedingly impatient.

Writtus reopened his scroll.

"Least serious of all, but nevertheless demanding royal disposition, is the matter of the large, semi-nude gentleman standing before Your Exaltedness clad only in assorted animal pelts and metal trinkets. His other chief item of apparel—a highly dangerous broadsword which he carries thonged at his waist without sheath—is in custody of the commander of the prison. This fellow states that he was shipwrecked and cast up on the shore of Atlantis. He has been making the rounds of the inns, causing turmoil wherever he goes. Further, he claims that in his native land, Chimeria—"

Geriasticus interrupted, "We have no knowledge of that principality."

"No, it isn't even on any of the maps," Writtus acknowledged.

"Pox on your map-makers!" screamed Conax. "Can I help it if those feeble-eyed fops are ignorant? I'd invite them to visit but the thin-blooded villains would surely freeze their privates the minute they crossed the borders of my noble northern nation!"

"He has a florid rhetoric," observed General Pytho. "Rather like the purple phrasing of the tellers of adventure tales, who swap their narratives for a tenth of a zeb a word in the scroll mart."

"But note those big, handsome muscles, General," said Num, flushing prettily. "Why don't we take him into protective custody too?"

"To continue," Writtus said officiously, "I personally find this foreigner guilty of no great crime. He only needs to settle the various due bills presented by the owners of inns whose fixtures he has destroyed at the slightest pretext. However, the disposition of his case falls within the purview of Your

52

Exaltedness because, as I started to say a while ago, he purports to be of royal lineage in his native land."

Conax shouted, "I understand little of this puling palaver. I'm a king, that's all—a king!" He emphasized it with several thumps of his fully-muscled chest. "Furthermore, I expect to be treated as one, else you'll rue it when my reavers rescue me!"

Fretting at the clamor, Geriasticus said, "We recognize no sovereign states more northerly than the duchies of Espaniozo. Therefore we can accord you no special treatment. Your case will be handled as a routine civil matter. Now, if the court will excuse us, we have other matters demanding our attention—"

And, upsetting one of the bowls of scented water at his feet, Geriasticus X attempted to leave the dais.

The king's answer wasn't good enough for Conax, however.

"Just one moment, shingle-shanks!"

Gasps of horror rose from the courtiers. Even General Pytho paled visibly.

"Are you saying that Conax the Chimerical speaks to you with a tongue with a fork in it? By Crok, my nose tells me it's you whose veracity smells!"

Geriasticus X became positively rigid. General Pytho popped up and pulled a dirk. Not to be cowed, Conax stamped forward.

"I have had a bellyful of these pretty, perfumed posturings You doubt I'm a king. I suppose you'll also doubt that I saw those selfsame lights in the sky which your milksop minions insist on denying."

At this, Geriasticus trembled.

"Also, you ivory-jawed hound of hell, one of those lighted specters descended to the sea where I and my reavers sailed in search of plunder. Instantly, through scarifying sorcery, it transformed itself into some species of ocean-going sea monster with luminous orbs. At the height of the storm which destroyed my proud vessel, it sailed off in plain view of every last drowning lad. Let any who dares call Conax a lynx-tongued liar step forward!"

"Hear, hear!" Babylos clapped. "At last, the fresh air of truth blows through this fetid domain!"

The cheeks and wattles of Geriasticus X had now changed from their normal waxy color to a mild pink—sign of great rage in one so enfeebled! Entirely forgetting his rank, the king tottered toward Conax. I immediately sensed a heating-up of the atmosphere, which I had been attempting to cool down with flattering remarks.

Heedless of the oaths and commands of the soldiers, I lost no time rushing to Conax myself. (Geriasticus was still in the process of inching his way across the floor!) I bent, catching a whiff of Conax's fur cloak—gamy, I don't mind telling you!

"Try to cool your rage," I whispered. "Otherwise you'll incur his full fury. You saw no lights!"

"By hell's maw, I did! Get away from me, you overweight bootlicker!"

"But Conax, it's a matter of survival—!"

Geriasticus pointed at the barbarian with a palsied hand.

"Recant! No omens glowed in our skies! Your eyes never beheld a single—"

"I won't be called a liar one more time!" And, seizing the nearest object—myself!—Conax picked it up and hurled it directly at the king!

Ah, how the gods frowned then! For in crashing into Geriasticus X—the ultimate affront upon his person!—somehow I managed to dislodge his ivory uppers. They went skittering and clacking across the throne room floor with an unnatural liveliness quite bizarre to behold.

The king and I toppled in a heap. With unbridled passion, Conax began grasping other objects—soldiers, courtiers, furniture, page boys, even Captain Num!—and hurling them in all directions, while he invoked Crok at the top of his lungs.

Aphrodisia screamed, Babylos cheered, courtiers fled, General Pytho swore, Captain Num fainted, and soldiers by the platoon leaped upon Conax and tried to subdue him. I last saw him going down under at least fifteen attackers, still punching and biting gamely.

I knew he'd caused the worst to happen when Geriasticus cried out:

"No civil sentences! No court appearances! Positively no appeals! Nothing but execution—*execution*—!"

"Your wish," purred General Pytho, "is my command."

So saying, he attacked me, and pummeled me unmercifully. Consciousness, as well as all hope, promptly faded away.

⋆ Six ⋆

O the wailing from Aphrodisia, when I woke with a throbbing pate to find myself in the selfsame dungeon from which I had journeyed to the throne room.

O the threats of physical harm from hot-tempered Conax!

O the lamentations of Babylos, certain now that the flashing heaven lights—not to mention their denial by the court!—signified dire times ahead.

I must confess that I shared his conviction. On the other hand, I wondered whether I really needed to worry. When one's head is to be lopped off, what matter the calamities of next week?

Stumbling up from my dizzy awakening—by night or day, who could tell in these foul cellars?—I found myself ringed by my fellow prisoners, all crying their various accusations.

Aphrodisia was the most direct of the lot.

"Basically, Hoptor, the fact that we're—(sniffle)—still here in this offal-smelling place is—(snuffle) your fault. So what are you going to (sob) do about it?"

A bit irritably, I advised her that I was first going to attempt to control my vertigo; second, soothe the pulsations in my limbs and temples by remaining as inactive as possible; and third, try to arrange with Menos to bring me something other than swill to fill my stomach.

"Still thinking of no one but yourself, eh?" With this, Conax gripped my throat and throttled me.

I waved my hands and rolled my eyes—my voice box would produce little more than gargles!—and, for once, Aphrodisia displayed a measure of sense.

"Really, Conax, for a supposed monarch, your behavior is disgraceful. How can Hoptor tell us what he plans when you're choking him to death?"

Conax digested this—applying pressure the while!—but then, with a grumble, released me. Massaging my throat to assuage the pain, I glowered at the Chimerical warrior.

"Did you honestly believe I would procure decent rations for myself and not share them with my cell companions?"

"Knowing you, very likely," said Conax, ever the cynic.

"That shows you how much you know about my character! Just rattle the bars, will you? Ask them to fetch me Menos straightaway. Though I'm in extreme pain due to bodily abuse, I intend to waste no time executing my plan to save us."

Aphrodisia said, "If it involves selling, renting, or otherwise trading on my body, Hoptor—"

"Fair warning!" I interrupted, a pacifying hand in the air. "Happily, it does not. Only I shall suffer personal debasement —in order to secure freedom and pardon for all!"

This statement was greeted with skeptical expressions. I chose to ignore them. Since no one had yet responded to my instructions to summon Menos, I took care of the job myself, screaming, gibbering, and otherwise behaving in a lunatic manner. That got action, I don't mind saying!

"Hoptor, Hoptor! Are you suffering a spasm? Is this your final extremity?"

Jumping up from the floor, I said, "Not a bit of it, Menos. That was merely my strategy for attracting your attention. Tell me at once—how long have we got?"

"Until I can scrape a death squad together. Tomorrow at the outside."

"Is it night or morning now?"

" 'Tis the morning after your audience."

At that, my aches ached worse than before; truly I had suffered hard blows, to remain unconscious such a long time!

Old leek-breath looked the very picture of a nervous man burdened with an unwelcome responsibility.

"I'd do anything within reason for you, Hoptor. But there is absolutely no means by which I can reverse the sentence of His Exaltedness. I can only delay it until sunrise, or, if I report my most experienced executioners suffering from an unexpected outbreak of flux, noon. Geriasticus does appreciate that a beheading calls for skill. None of that clumsy chopping and hacking! The blow must be powerful and clean, neatly severing—oh, sorry."

"We must be out of here by the morrow, Menos!"

"I wish I could help. But as I say, there's no way. Even your many debtors are powerless."

"Perhaps. But with my intimate knowledge of palace affairs, not to mention my keen awareness of the private pleasures—lusts!—of members of the court, I believe I know the one person who might be able to wind the king around her finger, and commute our sentence."

An expression of startlement appeared on his face. "You don't mean the queen?"

"Who else? Now, Menos, heed me well—"

I lowered my voice, conscious of the inquisitive stares of my cell-mates; especially the Chimerical king. He was busy cracking his knuckles loudly, and piercing me with optical daggers.

"In repayment for that favor we've discussed previously, I want you to get a message to Lady Voluptua."

"Any message must pass through that warthog who is in charge of her ladies."

"How you circumvent gross Swinnia is your problem. The message to be conveyed to the queen must be delivered exactly as I state it. In addition, it must be delivered today."

At that he blinked his good eye and shook his head.

"It's not as impossible as staying your beheading. But I'm still not certain I can—"

"If you don't," I returned, "I shall inform various guards down here of the anecdote of the pickle-shaped birthmark, to which I have thus far only alluded in veiled terms. By sunup, it will be the talk of every gossip-monger in Atlantis."

"Then my children will hear it! And my grandchildren! Nieces! Nephews!"

"The decision is strictly up to you, Menos."

Miserably, he agreed to do his best. Then he asked for the message.

"Merely make certain Lady Voluptua knows that Hoptor the Vintner seeks an audience, in order to inform her about a certain gentleman who has the physical prowess to increase her personal pleasure. Those are the key words, Menos—increase her personal pleasure."

"But what does it signify, Hoptor?"

"Given Geriasticus, our king, and given Lady Voluptua—a mere fraction of his age, with notorious appetites—if you cannot decipher what it means, then I can only say you will never rise to an executive position in the dungeon corps, for you are not a keen thinker. Believe me, the phrase is common palace parlance. It will reverberate within Lady Voluptua's mind like a struck gong. But let's not stand here chattering, when you could be about your mission. Away with you! And see that you bring an answer promptly!"

Grumbling, Menos took himself off up the corridor. My secretive smile, coupled with my absolute refusal to divulge anything about my plan—in case it failed!—granted me a welcome respite from the abuse of my fellow prisoners.

Menos returned after nightfall, bearing a lantern and shaking his head in amazement. As he unlocked the cell, he said:

"I am to escort you personally to the female wing of the palace."

"See, didn't I tell you? Merely mentioning my name in the right quarter has unleashed the engine of our salvation. Aphrodisia—Conax—you can stop worrying. Hoptor has come through again!"

Gathering my cloak around me, I marched out of the cell.

Menos, two soldiers, and I climbed stairs, then crossed a windswept yard where lanterns bobbed in the dark. Overhead, lightning flickered behind ebony clouds.

"I've been pondering your scheme," Menos said. "I can only conclude that you mean to play the pim—ah, offer Lady Voluptua a lover."

"Brilliant, brilliant! May we hurry and escape this fearful wind?"

"But exactly who do you have in mind? Yourself?"

"Enough conversation, Menos! I don't mean to grow hoarse shouting in this gale."

So saying, I preceded him rapidly up a circular stair through whose slit windows lightning glared again.

At the top of the stair, Menos ordered his soldiers to halt. We were to go the rest of the way alone.

Proceeding, the two of us passed through ornate doors blazoned with reprehensible representations of males and females disporting together. The motifs had been designed by Lady Voluptua, and rendered by a sculptor of depraved appetites; according to the popular accounts, anyway. No wonder Babylos railed against royal immorality!

We entered a dim, scented corridor where oil-wicks swam in ceramic bowls. From behind veiled doorways drifted the giggles of courtesans. Here and there too, I glimpsed a tempting haunch, or bosom, as various handmaids fleeted on mysterious, and probably illicit, errands.

As we approached yet another set of doors—these guarded by two immense eunuchs in loincloths—Menos grew visibly uneasy. I pressed him as to why.

"I am not entirely positive that Swinnia understood my message correctly, Hoptor. I believe she did, but I can't guarantee—"

Before he could say more, one of the eunuchs shrilled, "Who approaches the queen's virgin portals?"

58

"Hoptor the Vintner! I'm scheduled for an audience."

Both eunuchs sniffed, as if to show their contempt for rutting males. One said, "Yes, you're expected."

And with a swish of his wrist he flung one door open.

Leaving Menos to fend for himself, I entered a lavishly appointed chamber where tiny thrushes perched in cages, cushions covered the polished floor, and sweetmeats and wine waited on a taboret of gold. Alas, on an oversize cushion alongside this taboret, Swinnia awaited also.

"I beg your pardon," I said smoothly. "I was expecting Her Exaltedness—"

"So you're Hoptor the Vintner! You clever rascal! I've wanted to meet you for ever so long. And now, at last, it's come to pass. I hear you're a lively lover. At least the street gossip says so. Well, let's not waste time—"

And the obese horror began to waddle in my direction!

Swinnia's diaphanous gown not only revealed her most personal charms, but the immensity of her weight problem as well. The gown—of bridal pink!—could do nothing to conceal her moustache, however.

She patted my stomach—too fondly for my taste! Then she simpered:

"I'll wager you think that because I own the queen's ear, Hoptor, you can gain an advantage through me. Why, I'll bet you're hoping I will put in a word to help you earn a reprieve."

She simpered even more, while I stood utterly dumbfounded. I wished I had blundering Menos at hand. To murder. How had this unhappy twist of fate occurred?

"—Well, perhaps, after you spend an hour or two with me —after I discover whether you're as lively between the bedsheets as they say—perhaps *then* I might consider your cause. But not before, you sly fox!"

Another simper—O nauseating coyness! It was all I could do to reply, "I believe there has been some mistake, dear Swinnia—"

Ignoring the remark, she pinched me playfully.

"I hear you sell girls to noblemen! No wonder your passion is constantly running away with you. I'm not even in that type of trade, and my thoughts are always dwelling on—but never mind. I received your message. Not personally—I was taking my milk bath when it arrived. But one of my handmaidens interviewed old one-eye. I shouldn't admit it, but I was thrilled to learn that you wanted to come here tonight, and increase my personal pleasure. Naturally I understood that phrase, you dear thing—!"

And thereupon she grabbed me, and bore me to the cushions, kissing my cheeks and feverishly tampering with my garments!

To be honest, I doubted that anyone had increased Swinnia's personal pleasure in years. She was therefore wildly impatient. From my position beneath her sizable bulk, I exclaimed:

"Couldn't we sip a little wine first?"

"Later!" she gasped. "Later, you wicked boy—"

"Wait, wait! You must understand—"

"I understand *everything*, including the depths of your passion!"

"Yes," I squeaked, "passion—those are certainly a pair of beauties standing guard outside your doors."

That, mercifully, halted her fumblings. She reared up on hands and knees.

"The eunuchs?"

"Who else? I've never seen a more fetching twosome!"

"You—you—you prefer *gentlemen?*"

"Oh, yes, I have for years. Sad to say, I'm a confirmed eunuch-lover—to the despair of my parents, and lovely ladies like yourself who wish their personal pleasure increased."

What a dreadful falsehood to be wrung from the lips of Hoptor the Vintner! Yet it was either that, or possible death by exhaustion in the arms of this moustached behemoth.

Blowing a lock of hair from her eyes, Swinnia lumbered to her feet. She seized the platter of sweetmeats, dumping its contents on my head.

"Then go importune the guards, if that's your perverse preference!"

"One moment, my lady! You may heap abuse on me—not to mention edibles!—but I did wish to speak with your mistress, the queen."

"Out, out!" ordered Swinnia, quivering over every inch of her; indeed, her flesh was very nearly as active as Conax's, though not nearly so firm.

Immense tears began to drip from her eyes, muddling her cheek-paint as she continued:

"I've never been so outraged and demeaned in my life. The sooner they lop off your unnatural head, the better!"

Ah, Menos, wait till you're once more in my presence! I raged in silence, all the while maneuvering around Swinnia in a desperate attempt to keep from being shoved out.

O, her fury! She threw the wine jar. It smashed, making

a mess of the cushions. She was searching for something else to throw when, without warning, hangings on the room's far side were parted by a bangled arm.

"What is this noise that breaks our slumber?" Lady Voluptua demanded, hiding a yawn behind her hand.

"Merely a personal matter," Swinnia told her. "Out, Vintner, out—!"

Lady Voluptua blinked. "Who is that fat tradesman you're menacing, Swinnia?"

"None other than Hoptor the Vintner," I cried, abasing myself and knocking my forehead vigorously. "Come to seek private conversation with Your Exaltedness."

"The message was delivered to me by mistake." said Swinnia, casting vengeful glances at me. "However, it contained nothing of interest."

"Merely information on a new means for increasing your personal pleasure," I exclaimed.

"My personal—?" All at once she was wide awake. "Pleasure?"

Swinnia was wrath personified. "Don't listen to him, my lady! He has already confirmed that, because of his peculiar tastes, he couldn't increase the personal pleasure of a female pig!"

Now I seized the moment, heedless of Swinnia's glowers— for what harm could she do me if my head were severed from my body? I crawled toward the hem of Lady Voluptua's gown —straight through a wine-puddle, that being the fastest route —saying the while:

"The means of increasing Your Exaltedness' personal pleasure is not this humble person—oh no! It's another gentleman entirely. One with whom I don't believe you're acquainted. I sought an appointment to tell you about him. Through a chance misunderstanding, this worthy lady interpreted the message as meant for her."

"Someone new? For dalliance? Well—"

For a moment, Voluptua's bored look told me I had failed. Swinnia registered smug pleasure.

Then, however, a sort of superheated smile curled up the corners of the queen's mouth. She stretched in a maddeningly seductive way; she was raven-haired, and of staggeringly lush proportions. She wore a night dress which, by comparison, made Swinnia's seem a model of modesty.

She said, "It *might* be worth a moment or two of our time—"

"Oh, more than that, Your Exaltedness, I can promise!"

"Swinnia—"

"Yes, my lady?"

"Fetch more wine. Then leave us a while. We have nothing better to do—we've only been slumbering in utter boredom."

Swinnia was on the point of retorting. But since her mistress spoke with the calm arrogance of nobility, she didn't. She waddled into the shadows, emerging after a moment with another jar. She set it on the taboret with such force that I thought it would certainly shatter.

No, I would be the one to shatter, her eyes promised me, just before her size twelve slippers bore her away into the gloom.

"Here, sit near us, Vintner."

Voluptua plumped up cushions and sank down languorously. I had seen her before, of course, at various public ceremonial functions. In close-up, she was even more sensual and seductive.

She located a glass behind the taboret, and began to preen, saying:

"Hoptor—Hoptor—Hoptor the Vintner. It seems I recall you had an audience at court. You're to be executed, or something like that."

"Think nothing of it, my lady. I'm certainly not worrying!"

"Very well, if you say so. La! Life is so full of quirks!"

And she poured a jot of wine for herself, completely forgetting to offer me any.

I, however, was more than willing to overlook impoliteness in order to accomplish my mission.

"My lady, you already know something of my purpose—"

"Yes—" She ran a painted hand down one thinly-clad limb. "And we haven't had our personal pleasure increased in jus ages. What a thoughtful citizen you are, Hoptor, to concern yourself with the welfare of your queen."

"Fair Atlantis above all, my lady! Though I hope I will be forgiven for saying it, certainly it's no secret that His Exalted ness, the king, is so occupied with weighty matters of state craft that he often leaves the most luxurious flower in his garden untended."

"And when he does pay us a visit every few months, he does nothing but sleep all night, rattling those ivory teeth between whistles and snores!"

"Heavy are the burdens of kingship!" I intoned.

"Heavier still the burdens of being young—eager for personal pleasure's increase."

And she looked at me in such a smoky way that I very nearly fled from the chamber.

Of course I soon overcame such petty scrupling. Who is one human being to deny another satisfaction of his or her appetites? Especially when my life is at stake?

Voluptua gripped my hand. "Tell me, Vintner. Who is the hot-blooded stallion seeking entrance to these perfumed meadows?"

"Well, Your Exaltedness, to be perfectly frank, he isn't exactly seeking entrance yet. Rather, I think it need go the other way round. You must invite him. Considering your heaven-sent charms, I believe he will be instantly won."

"We do not ask lovers to come to us!"

"Yes, but this fellow's a huge, handsome rogue from northern Chimeria. He's unfamiliar with our courtly ways. He also has thews this big around."

"How big?" she exclaimed.

"This big," I said, increasing the space between my hands considerably. "The gentleman—Conax by name—being a stranger to fair Atlantis—would never think to force himself into your presence. This despite the fact he's a king in his own land."

"Chimeria, you say? I seem to recall some mention of a chap from there breaking furniture—"

"The very same chap!"

"Oh! They told me his thews were indeed immense!"

"Magnificent!" I replied, increasing the width between my hands even more. "And since he is a king, it would not demean your high station to issue the invitation. It would be a meeting of equals, so to speak."

Then—cleverly, I must admit!—I managed to feign an air of diffidence. Rising and bowing, I continued:

"However, it was merely a thought, Exaltedness. A token offered in respect for your skills in queencraft. For Hoptor a loyal citizen if nothing else! Now, having done his deed, our humble servant begs to conclude the interview."

She nibbled at her moist lower lip, then searched me with another sultry gaze.

"We suppose there would be no harm in inviting this Conax to our chambers—"

"None at all! If you don't like what you see—that is, the choice is entirely yours. Accept him or reject him—after you see him. He's currently charged with some minor misdemeanor in connection with that broken furniture—" A wave. "But a word from you will surely open his cell."

"And do you have some sort of vested interest in all this, Hoptor?"

"Only the satisfaction of performing my patriotic duty. Oh, yes, there is the small sum of zebs Conax has paid me I serve as his official tutor and adviser on civilized manners and customs. But that's only a means to while away the hours in my cell."

Another stretch, and her verdict:

"We thank you, Hoptor the Vintner. We shall certainly entertain your suggestion most seriously. Perhaps tomorrow evening—"

I blurted, "What's wrong with tonight?"

"What's that?"

"Forgive our persistence, but there's a storm brewing outside. This is an ideal night for remaining indoors with—leisurely pursuits."

A peal of thunder reinforced the idea most opportunely The lustful minx was quick to decide.

"A point well taken. His Exaltedness always stays safely under the covers during inclement weather. The dampness makes his bones ache. We would not be disturbed. Very well we shall issue an invitation to this Chimerical prince tonight And bless you, Hoptor—you are a thoughtful, high-minded citizen!"

Admiring herself in the glass, she disappeared into the shadows.

Corrupt persons can think only of themselves, I decided retreating swiftly from the chamber in order to avoid further intercourse with Swinnia. I only hoped that the succeeding stages of my plan would not go awry, for I was sure the wicked queen would be taken with Conax; he was not unhandsome in a rough-edged sort of way.

And if love blossomed this night, I might present myself—Aphrodisia and Babylos, too—as members of the new favorite's retinue. Save one, save all, that was my theory.

A thin hope, you might conclude. But I had none fatter And time was running out.

In order to light my way on the stairs, I begged a torch from one of the eunuchs. I was informed that guards awaited in the courtyard to escort me back to my cell.

The wind howled through the slot windows. Lightning crackled frequently. As thunder boomed, a sudden gust extinguished my torch.

I stumbled on, bumping against someone—a shadow-shape

64

"All pardon," I said, not knowing whether I had encountered lord or lackey. "Please excuse my clumsiness—"

As I made to go around lightning fumed yet again. My eyes flew wide at the sight of the head rising from a mufti cowl.

With a shriek. I fled on down toward the courtyard.

Now indeed I knew that Babylos spoke truth, and that terrible, not to say supernatural, punishment would soon be visited on Atlantis.

The horrific reason remained burned in my memory. Above the cowl, I had glimpsed immense, elongated eyes seated in an angular face of purest, brightest blue.

A strange, foreign, phantasmagorical face—nothing of this world!

Yet I had touched the shadow-shape's solid reality—

I burst into the courtyard as the storm broke, eager for the protection of the soldiers, and rueing the day I'd sold my first vintage. Why hadn't I listened to Mother, who had wanted me to take up a respectable profession?

✳ Seven ✳

"Next to dispatching demons to the pits of perdition, my favorite sport is bouncing buxom, bumptious wenches—provided, of course, there's no permanent liaison involved. For once, hog-stomach, you have apparently done something right."

With this statement, Conax the Chimerical agreed to answer the summons of Lady Voluptua.

I had already reminded him that, per my earlier discussion, I had arranged matters so that we might win reprieve from the headsman. I also pointed out that he now bore the responsibility of capitalizing upon my gains.

Whereupon, he rose in my estimation—not far, mind you!—by readily accepting the duty, via the comment previously quoted.

Babylos and Aphrodisia begged to know what plot I was hatching, but I still said nothing to either of them. I was not anxious to subject myself to ridicule should the scheme misfire and we end up on the block after all.

I positioned myself next to the bars. As the rest of the cell row fell into silence, I nervously counted the tickings of time, awaiting the thump of booted feet on the stair.

An hour passed. Then another. I began to despair.

All at once, tramp-tramp, a squad of plug-uglies appeared, rain-sodden and out of sorts. Their leader ordered Conax unloosed.

"And I also," I said, insinuating myself into the cell doorway. Snapped the soldier in charge, "We have no orders concerning you."

"But I'm his tutor! He goes nowhere without me, fearing to inadvertently break some local rule and offend the Atlantean gods. Isn't that right, O mightly monarch of Chimeria?" I gigged Conax in the ribs.

"Oh, yes, right," he responded with a witless grin. "I go no place without this fat—uh, my tutor."

Thus, we marched.

Upstairs again; then across the courtyard in the downpour. The weeping sky reminded me of the apparition I had glimpsed earlier. Through effort, I had managed to put it from my mind, for intervals as long as two or three minutes. Now, however, I felt another shudder course along my spine, and I pondered the conundrum of the origin of that blue horror which had gazed at me in the lightning's flare.

I had never given much credence to the notion of gods and goddesses, though naturally I made obeisance, just in case. But now I wondered whether the blue manifestation could be some deity made finite.

Yet why would a god or goddess descend to Atlantis in a guise certain to terrify the inhabitants because of its very strangeness? I could in no wise begin to unravel the eerie mystery.

A dash of rain in my face helped take my mind off the subject. The high winds, furious thunderclaps, and other disturbances which heralded the arrival of a storm had since passed on, leaving only steady rain. Damp, I once more climbed that winding, windy stair—full of nothing more than shadows now, thanks be!

I got as far as the chamber in which I had spoken with Voluptua. Conax was passed on to dim inner quarters. But I was barred by my several-hundred-pound nemesis.

"No partisans of Graek love wanted in there!" Swinnia advised.

66

"But, my lady, I must attend him! I am his tutor in local ways. Should he start to commit a gross error, I would advise him before he incurred the queen's displeasure."

"Not without getting past me, you won't advise him."

"Please, dear Swinnia! Admit me and I'll make it up to you some way, I—"

Inspiration!

"—I promise to call upon you privately, at a time that is mutually convenient."

"What for?"

"To beg your assistance!"

"I'll arrange no midnight meetings with eunuchs!"

"Swinnia, you misunderstand! I am not happy in my state. You could help me regain my rightful role as a male. I believe your charms could at last rouse my indifference—"

"Oh, you're just trying to wheedle me."

I was, but I denied it.

"I'm sick of the netherworld of eunuchs and dandies who must creep out by night on matters illicit. Restore me, O bounteous lady! Restore me to the enjoyment of embraces of the opposite sex!"

"Well," she said at length, "I *might* be able to help you. I do know many of the techniques of the courtesans—"

And once more I realized that Hoptor had read his opposition aright. In fact, the stout lady was breathing quite rapidly. The thought of a gentleman—any kind of gentleman, no matter what his persuasion—frenzied her to a fever pitch. Breathing in a labored way, she propelled me toward a doorway.

"Dart in—quickly, before Her Exaltedness arrives. Position yourself behind the first of the two lacquered screens. Heed me, now—the first screen, on your right hand. The one on the left is for another purpose. Be quiet as a grave robber, and when and if Lady Voluptua and your handsome friend retire, we shall go immediately to my rooms. I'll see what I can do about rescuing you from your condition."

Pushing through the hangings, I discovered a chamber even larger and more luxurious than the first. It lacked one wall, however, the open space giving onto a large terrace. Undoubtedly the queen took the air out there in better weather. At the moment, nothing much could be seen save sheets of rain cascading from the eaves above.

Despite being open on one side, the room was not cold. On the contrary, it was stupefyingly hot, thanks to a row of braziers set along the terrace opening.

Upon seeing me, Conax—the very picture of barbaric

splendor in his many-pelted cape and pieces of body-jewelry—started to blurt out some remark. A finger at my lips cautioned him to silence.

Quickly, I slipped behind the nearest lacquered screen, noting an identical one on the room's far side.

A gong rang, rather tinnily. Lady Voluptua appeared at an inner portal.

The queen was garbed as I had seen her last. But she had applied fresh eye-black, and her perfume would have staggered a statue. She slinked—that is the only proper term for it—to the center of the room, barely able to keep her eyes off her guest's bulging biceps.

Conax glanced worriedly in my direction. I put my lips to one of the screen's scrolled cutouts and started to whisper, "Abase yourself—!"

But Lady Voluptua forestalled this bit of protocol.

"You needn't kneel, since you are reportedly a king in your own right. And let's not waste time on other formalities."

She linked her arm with his, dimpling in a way I found scandalous for one of supposedly so exalted a station.

"Our bed chamber lies beyond those curtains. It's ever so much nicer for a get-acquainted chat—"

Knowing precisely what sort of chat she had in mind—had I not coached the Chimerical one to the best of my ability?—Conax rippled his thews, thereby shrugging off her clinging touch.

"What, acting the coy rogue with us?" Lady Voluptua said. I feared the game was over before it had begun.

But my tiresome repetition of the same statements—I had spoken them as many as three and four times each to Conax, without variation!—now yielded a harvest.

"Coy? No, Crok attest—never with a wench so sensuously seductive as yourself. However, you have got to remember that I have other things on my mind which may distract me, and affect my performance of—uh, performance," he concluded, with another helpless glance at the screen. Perhaps he was at home with buxom, bumptious wenches, but the presence of a hot-eyed royal temptress seemed to confound him.

"Pardon!" I hissed through the screen.

"Pardon?" he repeated.

"What did you do?" Lady Voluptua wanted to know. Then, switching her hips, she teased his chin with one finger. "La! So far, nothing."

"Oh, by Crok, I see—*pardon!*"

Voluptua stamped a jeweled slipper. "Are you repeating

that stupid word merely to be vexatious? If you have some-thing on your mind that is going to interfere with our get-acquainted chat, we wish you'd get it off your not incon-siderable chest."

It took Conax a moment to unwind the meaning of that statement. But, mercifully, he did.

"My lady, it is simply that being here with you—such a dazzling, delicious damsel—is pleasure partially dimmed be-cause I'm scheduled to have my head cut off. As the rightful ruler of Chimeria, I'm damned mad about it, too. When my reavers—oh." He was recalling my stiff warning about threats, no doubt.

"So you're another one due for execution? Like your friend the tutor?"

"That's right. Personally, I can't see that my crime was all that great. I did nothing but break a few pieces of furniture, which in Chimeria is regarded as a sign of a mature, warlike temperament. Of course, I can't properly judge the crimes of those others—especially that overweight so-called wine sell-er—"

Oh, the impudent, scheming lout! Conax had proved himself more wily than I suspected. It made no difference that, in his position, I would have behaved in precisely the same way.

From my vantage point behind the screen, however, I was furious.

"—But I don't see why, as one member of royalty to an-other, you can't agree to speak to that old—ah, your hus-band, and inquire about having my sentence set aside."

"Conax," I whispered. *"Conax, you traitor—!"*

"Is someone calling your name from without?" Lady Vo-luptua asked.

The Chimerical one had heard me clearly. I thought I detected a flush of shame on his cheeks. As well I should! He said:

"Uh, naturally, if you can also encourage the king to pardon Hoptor and the others who share my cell, I'm sure they would be grateful. But here on the verge of what promises to be a fine get-acquainted chat, I just can't bring myself to fully chatting trim unless I have at least your verbal assurance that you'll do what you can."

"In other words, your performance is contingent upon peace of mind?"

"By Crok, yes. Single-minded, that's the sort of king I am."

Manipulating his thews with her perfumed hands, Lady

69

Voluptua breathed, "Yes, yes, all right, we shall discuss the matter—"

"With the king?"

"With the king, with the king! But in the morning. If we continue this endless talk about your fate, it *will* be morning."

"Very well," Conax returned. "Since I have your assurance, I am now ready to get acquainted."

And he allowed himself to be led straight toward a veiled doorway.

Just then, with everything finally going well, there was another abrupt reversal.

From directly above the terrace beyond the braziers, a blinding light shone down. For a heartbeat I fully expected to hear thunder. But there was no sound save for the outcry of a eunuch on guard somewhere outdoors. He scampered to the center of the terrace and pointed upward into the light's heart. All at once he threw away his spear, rushed to the parapet, jumped up and hurled himself into oblivion.

In a trice, the terrifying sight he'd seen began to reveal itself to those of us inside.

Lady Voluptua cried for her guards. Several rushed in. But after one glance at the source of the unearthly radiance, they rushed right out again.

Through the rain, I heard halloos and alarms. The light had been glimpsed by more than just those of us quavering in Voluptua's quarters. As we watched, petrified with horror, the wellspring of the radiance dropped down into full view. I in turn dropped to my knees, making hasty repentance of all my sins.

"Dragon ship!" Conax bawled. "The same as stood by and watched my war craft founder! See its hell-bright eyes—?"

They seemed to me not eyes but peculiar ovoid lanterns, fixed to one end of the craft that lowered soundlessly toward the terrace, glowing in a penumbra of light. Tripod legs popped from its underbelly.

The phantasm was shaped somewhat like a hen's egg, with the running lanterns at the larger end. A peculiar spine-like affair protruded from its upper surface. A rippling, iridescent pattern seemed embedded in its silvery outer skin. The resemblance to a dragon s head was only superficial.

Was this one of the devices which had sped glowing through the heavens above the prison?

"Forward, you cowards, on penalty of death!" Lady Voluptua exclaimed. A handful of soldiers said their final prayers aloud, and charged the glowing artifact.

They whacked it with swords, jabbed it with spears, assaulted it with oaths of the strongest sort. For several moments this idle fray continued. Then, from the innards of the device, there issued a loud clacking.

A section of its patterned shell opened, falling outward and down like a trick door hinged at the bottom. From this opening there appeared an incline; to be more accurate, the incline appeared to grow out of the edge of the down-hanging door. When the incline touched the terrace, the clacking noise ceased.

The device continued to shed its unearthly radiance, illuminating the soldiers, who had given up their vain attack and were hurling themselves from the parapet or falling upon their own swords.

It is better testament to the inept leadership of fair Atlantis—I include General Pytho in a preeminent position!—that not one of the soldiers succeeded in dispatching himself.

All at once—wonder upon wonders—a being, or person, appeared in the opening in the lighted device. And I had seen its counterpart elsewhere!

The visitor touched a fur-clad toe to the incline. It then proceeded to glide down the steep, smooth slope without aid or falter. It wore a full-length cloak of glowing material. The cowl was thrown back. From the collar region there arose a largish head with inquisitive but not necessarily hostile eyes.

Those eyes were oversized, and elongated. Further, every exposed inch of the unnerving figure was blue!

I cannot begin to capture the tumult of the first moments of that encounter. Suffice it to say, every eye in Lady Voluptua's chamber was fixed upon the new arrivals. A second one had appeared, and was gliding down the incline while the first opened its mouth to taste the falling rain with a livid blue tongue. If it was annoyed, it gave no sign.

Three additional beings emerged. When all had negotiated the incline, they marched forward toward the row of braziers.

By this time, military reinforcements had arrived, taken stock of the situation, and were now huddled together in the corner, shield clanking and clinking against shield. The pack swelled—first a squad, then a platoon.

"Hell's holy harpies! I'll not be unmanned by a pack of flesh-curdling phantoms!"

With this announcement, mighty Conax ran to one of the braziers. Scattering coals willy-nilly, he hauled it up over his head and hurled it at the blue beings.

The foremost of these caught the brazier in two swiftly-

71

raised, long-fingered hands. It bent the metal into a twist, then threw it away with the speed of a projectile.

I stoutly deny, as Conax later accused, that I let out a feminine scream. The scream issued from the other screen, which toppled over simultaneously with mine.

As I dashed for the chamber door, I saw coming at me with equal speed those who had been likewise hidden—General Pytho and Captain Num. The latter's weepings could be heard above all else.

"Oh, I'll never forgive you for enticing me into this horrid situation, General. And all in order to gain favor with that drity old man! Watch out, whoever you are, or I'll scratch your eyes out!"

This last was directed at me. Num went whizzing by, his curly locks flying.

Due to his haste, he completely failed to recognize me. At once I guessed that the general and his plaything had bribed Swinnia and insinuated themselves behind the second screen, in order to spy upon Voluptua. No doubt they planned to report her loose behavior to the king. What some would not do in order to secure favor and advancement!

Another roar spun me around.

"Don't be a fool, Conax!" I exclaimed. "Leave those nightmares alone—"

Useless warning!

With an ululating howl, Conax the Chimerical rushed onto the terrace. Heedless of his personal safety, he began to box and batter the blue beings with his bare hands. Such a temper!

✳ Eight ✳

It must be said of Conax that he did not shrink from doing battle with the blue beings, even though they stood a head taller than he. Their considerable height was accentuated by their slenderness and, despite my state of consternation, I was struck by the composed way in which they received the barbarian's batterings.

He whacked them with his doubled fists. He leaped in the

air and shot out one leg to deliver a stiff kick. He danced round them, uttering his ululating cry and gnashing his teeth. But he seemed neither to dismay nor harm the peculiar creatures.

"Fight, fight, what's the matter with you?" he protested, in a veritable fury of frustration. He crushed one of his big feet down upon the toe of a blue being. Even this produced no response.

They did react, however, when Conax attempted to gouge one's eye socket.

The blue being thus attacked seized Conax's thumb and bent it backward.

Conax dropped to his knees, grimacing. The gougee reached down, entwined blue fingers in Conax's locks, and, as if the Chimerical outlander were of a feather's weight, picked him up by the hair and threw him back in the room.

I leaped out of the way to avoid being struck. Lucky for Conax, cushions were available to break his fall, or he might have snapped his neck when he landed.

After wiping its fingers upon its garment—barbarians employ rendered fats as hair dressing, Conax had informed me—the attacked one signed to its mates. One by one, the blue beings ascended the incline.

All the foregoing transpired in but a fraction of the telling time. During the same interval, I discovered, Lady Voluptua had vanished entirely. So had the yellow-backed Captain Num. General Pytho, however, had remained, though he had positioned himself to the rear of the soldiers huddling behind their shield wall.

Stunned Conax reeled this way, then that, boxing empty air in the hope of finding an enemy. General Pytho ordered his minions to cast their spears. One fellow did so, just as the last of the blue beings ascended to its craft.

The spear sailed through the rain, and I felt certain it would strike with mortal force in the blue phantasm's backbone— if backbones they had!

But, as if warned by some internal sense, the creature turned.

Extending one hand, it caught the spear in mid-air. It drew the weapon up close to examine it. No expression readable by mortal men crossed its face. But from the way it ultimately cast the spear aside, it clearly considered the weapon harmless.

The blue creature vanished inside the glowing device. Clacking, the incline began to draw itself upward. Soon the outer shell was again unbroken.

I dashed to where Conax was still hopping and capering, and attempted to seize his arm—no mean feat! I earned a punch in the pate for my pains, and only captured his attention by hanging doggedly on one wrist.

"Kindly recover your senses, Conax! You're fighting empty air!"

I noticed that his eyes—bloodshot with barbaric fury—failed to focus.

"I'll teach them to humiliate a red ruffian of the north!"

"Calm yourself! And quickly!" I was all too aware of General Pytho peeping at me from behind the clump of soldiers. The assorted scars on his face purpled simultaneously. More trouble on the way!

"You, Vintner! Stand fast! Also your muscle-bound ally! From my position behind that fallen screen, I witnessed your pathetic attempt to curry favor. As commander-in-chief, I inform you that your ploy has failed. I intend to return you to the dungeon straightaway. Whether dead or breathing depends entirely on your attitude."

Conax looked at Pytho in a somewhat cross-eyed way. "What jerk-kneed jackal of hell yaps now—?"

"Our captor," I informed him. And then, because matters could in no wise become worse, I added, "I know back ways if we gain the streets. Let's cut for it!"

"Charge them! Surround them! Seize them!" Pytho screamed.

Before the cowed soldiers could obey, I grabbed cushions from the floor, throwing them with all my might.

Taking my cue, Conax got hold of another brazier. With a stout heave, he sailed it through the air.

The soldiers suffered a rain of pillows and hot coals. Then a sword sliced through one pillow, creating a veritable maelstrom of goose feathers.

Landing upon glowing coals, some of the feathers caught fire. Recoiling, all the soldiers shifted backward, squeezing General Pytho against the wall. From this awkward position he issued orders impotently.

Picking up the hem of my cloak, I cried, "Follow me, Conax!" and dashed away.

Racing through the room where I had met Voluptua earlier, I heard clamor from far and near. Gongs rang. Boots hammered. Men swore. Women shrieked. The entire female wing was in a state of insane disorder, even though a hasty glance backward showed the glowing craft already rising upward.

I plucked a plumed helmet from a fainted soldier. As General Pytho continued to call for pursuit, I blew out the last two lamps in the chamber, thrust the carved doors open and rushed through.

"Gods protect us!" I exclaimed. "The invaders are slaughtering everyone! General Pytho orders full retreat!"

Per my plan, the two eunuchs only caught a glimpse of my helmet as I whizzed past them with all possible speed. Burly Conax was right on my heels. We had gone about half the distance to the winding stair before the eunuchs realized there was something amiss with a soldier whose uniform consisted of a helmet and common robe.

Their frenzied yells merely added to the din.

We'd gone but part way down the stair when we encountered another squad of armed men coming up.

Two carried firebrands. I politely pointed the way.

"Hurry, General Pytho has his back to the wall!"

"Forward, men, to the relief of our beloved leader!"

As they rushed up, we rushed down.

Soon, negotiating the last flight, we reached the courtyard. More soldiers ran to and fro. Some bore torches. All demanded to know what was happening. For good reason: the female wing gave off the sounds of a battlefield. Oaths. Commands. Countercommands, crashes, and additional ringing gongs. Over all, a flashing speck, the ascending dragon craft diminished in size.

Even as I watched, it reached its apex, zipped to the right, and disappeared behind scudding rain clouds.

"How do we get back to the dungeons, Hoptor?"

"For a king, you're certainly not the brightest. Naturally we're not going back to the dungeons!"

"By Crok, your logic eludes me. Did we not agree, in those slime-ridden depths, to seek release of the girl and that old prattler? How can we ignore such a vow without besmirching our honor?"

"See here, Conax. We can be far more useful in effecting the rescue if we operate outside the palace confines." As I spoke, I tugged him toward a courtyard gate. Happily, we were all but ignored by the confused, hallooing soldiery.

"The minds of you soft-bellied southerners are certainly confounding," he remarked.

"I appreciate your views. But just remember the slogan

75

is, when in Atlantis, do as the Atlanteans do. Look sharp now! We still have those nasties by the gate to deal with."

I referred to two guards stationed in a booth. Though obviously alarmed by the noise and heavenly lights, they had not as yet deserted their posts. And the area round their booth was brightly lit, thanks to a wormwood torch in a wall socket.

"Here, you look more like a soldier than I do. Put this on and run ahead of me."

So saying, I shoved the helmet down on Conax's head. He complained bitterly about the earpieces gouging his temples.

We closed the distance to the booth. While we were still outside the perimeter of the torchlight, I bellowed:

"Quick, all troops to the female wing! General Pytho's order—the situation's desperate!"

As I pulled Conax to a halt, the guards fingered their hilts uncertainly.

"Hail, soldier!" said the foremost, eyeing Conax's mighty muscles. "Do you know you're out of uniform?"

"He knows it, he knows it," I responded. "His breastplates were torn off by the very enemy now pressing General Pytho to a last stand."

While saying this, I unsocketed the torch and thrust it into the soldier's hand.

"I too had my armor ripped away. I was forced to cover my shame with the first available garment. Make haste—and prepare to die gloriously. Those are direct orders from the general!"

They rushed off. But alas, they only went a short distance before stopping.

They turned back scrutinizing Conax and myself—with obvious suspicion!

I tugged frantically on the gate-rope while the pair continued conversing. The gate squealed up and I caught a whiff of street garbage—o precious exhalation of Atlantean freedom!

The guards flourished their swords, shouting, "Stand fast, there! In the name of Geriasticus—!"

"This way!" I shrieked, virtually jerking Conax off his feet.

Thus we pelted out of the palace enclosure, the two guards raising hue and cry not far behind.

We flashed up circuitous streets and down paved avenues. From time to time it seemed as if we had outdistanced our pursuers. Then a glint of lanterns and a flare of firebrands in-

76

dicated otherwise. They were still coming on, in even larger numbers than before.

The streets were all but abandoned. The rain, though slacked to a drizzle, kept all but the most hardy or criminous indoors. Thus, while our flight was unimpeded, my own bulk proved our greatest handicap.

My progress grew less fleet each moment. My chest darted with the pains of overexertion. But somehow I kept on.

At length, having dodged the hounds for almost an hour, we found ourselves within a block of my villa. From a second story apartment balcony to which we'd clambered, we observed that a contingent of military had already arrived.

Soldiers milled at my front door. Others made free with the interior, if I could judge from the shouts issuing therefrom. Talk about lack of respect for property!

"Well," I panted, "refuge in my home is out. Let us think—"

"While you do so, I'm going to sit on this rail and rest. Even I, accustomed to trailing brigands, mercenary invaders, and magically propelled imps for hours on end, am somehow wearied by this banging around in the dark."

"Not half so wearied as—'ware that flowerpot—!"

Too late! The pot crashed into the street.

Inside, the owner of the apartment fired a lamp.

"Robbers, robbers! Under the beds or we'll be murdered!"

Alas, sharp-eared soldiers had heard the pot shatter. And none could help hearing the apartment owner's outcries. The soldiers swarmed toward us in the street. That left only the apartment.

I crashed through the hangings, Conax at heel, and came face to face with an old fellow in a night-stocking.

Putting on a fearsome face, I shrieked, "Your zebs or your life!"

Dropping his lamp, he fainted.

We blundered around an assortment of furniture, raced down a smelly stair reeking of supper cabbage, and escaped via the decayed structure's back door.

"Rotten Row," I gasped. "Follow me!"

But it soon appeared that we might not reach our goal. My steps and those of Conax were flagging badly Moreover, the soldiers seemed to be everywhere at once, squads of them, companies of them, hallooing, waving lights, and cuffing anyone who crossed their path.

Entering one street, for example, we were forced to retreat hastily on sight of a squad marching toward us. Stumbling down an alley, we glimpsed a similar contingent ahead We

77

rushed through the first floor of an adjacent building, and into the street beyond, while I grew concerned about the scope of General Pytho's pique. That he would devote such effort in pursuit of my insignificant, harmless person did not augur well. It was also further evidence of the wrongful priorities of the Island Kingdom's leadership!

"We'll never escape at this rate," Conax puffed. "There's armor everywhere!"

"Pray what (gasp) do you suggest?"

"Well, I'd as lief halt and make my death-stand, taking a dozen of the snapping dogs with me to the nether regions. In fact—" He planted his great feet in place. "I believe I will."

"Are you out of your barbaric mind? What if they don't kill you, but overcome you? Do you want to go back to the dungeon?"

"Come to think of it, I believe we should. As I announced earlier, I don't feel quite right leaving the others locked up while we run around all over the city..Not that I have any special attachment for the soothsayer and your baggage. But we did include them in our plans—"

"And we'll rescue them yet! Unless you persist in engaging in philosophic hairsplittings about worthless commodities such as honor, in which case we'll surely be caught."

"But flight is profitless, Hoptor! See that sign over there?"

He directed my attention to a hanging board. It fronted the shuttered shop of one Pittos, the Fig Vendor.

"We have already passed that sign four times. You're simply running around in circles!"

"I am trying to locate a hiding place on Rotten Row!"

"It appears you can't even locate Rotten Row itself."

"Conax, will you please—oh-oh. Another military mob, just a block off. They've spotted us! Now you've done it—!"

I decided then and there to abandon Conax to his own mad devices. If he wished to be seized, that was up to him. But I was determined to make one final, brave effort to gain the security of Rotten Row. Its denizens would surely conceal us in their midst.

So deciding, I ran.

I had gone but a few wobbly paces when I found the barbarian panting at my side. As we slipped and slathered along a twisty way, I inquired:

"What (pant) changed your mind?"

"I wanted to ask you a question."

"More philosophic quibbles! Here, to the right—Rotten Row can't be more than two blocks away."

"I (puff) have encountered (puff), as I believe I have re-marked (pant), warlocks, demons, and monsters without number, during (gasp) the course of my barbaric career. But I have never—upon my stars, never!—witnessed such a sight as I saw at the palace. What (puff) were those blue devils, anyway?"

"A visitation of the wrath of the gods? Mummers preparing for a performance? In heaven's name, how should I know? At the moment, I'm not the least interested. My own skin is my main—"

At that exact moment, I ceased speaking, and my spirits fell to their lowest point of the night.

Directly ahead, the darkened street which we were traversing opened directly onto a cross-thoroughfare. On its opposite side rose the dives of Rotten Row.

But its denizens would offer us no sanctuary this night. Those denizens were being herded out of the various establishments by yet another company of Pytho's soldiers. Even little Mimmo was being manhandled!

Heartsick, I halted in the shadow a few steps from the street's end. Suddenly a shape glided from a black doorway, stomach foremost.

"Care for a little entertainment, stranger? Half-price special in effect tonight only—"

"Rhomona! Why are you on the streets?"

"I haven't had time to arrange for that short loan as yet. And I can't get a single customer, even by offering bargain rates. Careful, Hoptor, not too close to the light! Those soldiers have turned the town upside-down."

"Of that I am well aware."

"You realize they're all searching for you. I've never before seen such an extensive manhunt."

"When General Pytho succumbs to a fixation," I sighed, "he truly succumbs."

"Who's your handsome, muscular friend?" she asked, casting her eyes over Conax's thews.

"Never mind, I've no time for introductions. Gods preserve me, Rotten Row was our last hope!"

Conax hitched up his clout and flexed his fingers into claws. "Since that refuge is plainly gone, I am going to march out there and make my death-stand. May Crok guide me to his sacred, scented bowers, freighted on the raging red river of the blood of my enemies!"

"For mercy's sake, Conax, not again—!"

"I hate to say it, Hoptor," remarked Rhomona, "but a last

79

ditch fight may be your only alternative. General Pytho's men have informed everyone that you are to be executed on sight. I can't think of a single safe hiding place, short of your jumping in the sea."

"You're absolutely right. My villa is surrounded, the Bloody Bench is unavailable, even—*Rhomona!*"

"What?" she cried, sorely alarmed.

"Rhomona, you have repaid Hoptor the Vintner tenfold!" Thereupon I seized her, and bussed her cheek.

Then I lunged after the tag end of Conax's cloak, catching it an instant before he reached the cross-street.

"Wait, wait, don't make your death-stand yet! I have an idea."

"What is it this time? If it's like all your other schemes, it probably won't work."

"Yes, I believe it will. Rhomona, run out there and keep their attention diverted. My friend and I are going to clamber up yonder outside stair. If we go via the rooftops, it's but four squares to the seawall."

I gave the wench a shove, and she waddled into the light, immediately attracting the attention of the soldiers because of her advanced condition. Conax scampered after me up the staircase.

Following numerous hairbreadth adventures while crossing various tiled and slated roofs—at least up there, we met no members of the military!—we reached the great Island Kingdom wall.

We came down from the roofs near one of the mighty stone control wheels. When turned by a gang, each wheel revealed an opening—a valve—through which flood waters could rush out at low tide.

A few paces past the stone wheel, we climbed a public stair to the wall's summit, descending by a similar stair on the other side.

And there, exactly where I had hoped they would be, we found the small open boats of the Atlantean fishermen beached for the night among nets and pots on the reeking sand.

I selected the most seaworthy, hauled it into the foaming surf, and immediately clambered in. The tiny vessel threatened to capsize.

By jiggling one way and then another, I managed to balance it. Conax dutifully jumped in too, while I began to ply the oars.

"Where are we going?" he wanted to know.

Wondering again about the intelligence necessary to be

named a king in Chimeria, I retorted, "Why, on a pleasure cruise to the Isles Below the Wind. Where do you think we're going? We're going out to sea! We shall row around for a day, and perhaps by tomorrow night, it will be safe to return to shore. I remind you—perilous though the sea may be, we have no other safe haven."

"But we're liable to meet sea monsters and other demons of the deep."

"If so, it will give you a splendid opportunity to make your death-stand."

"You have a point," he agreed, settling back on his bench. "However. you will have to do all the rowing. In Chimeria, a king does not perform manual labor."

∗ Nine ∗

Happy to put the beach and its rotting fish-heads behind— not to mention possible search parties!—I plied the oars as vigorously as my strength would permit. To be perfectly honest, one does not develop stout muscles in the vintner's trade— except in that portion of the brain devoted to sharp bargaining!

Therefore, when we were a sufficient distance from the narrow necklace of beach which ringed fair Atlantis, I stepped the splintery mast. After I had installed the tiller in its socket, I handed a line to Conax and took up my position in the stern.

"What am I supposed to do with this rope?"

"Don't you know anything about sailing?"

"I am a king! My sailing master handles those mundane details."

"I see. Well, do nothing until I instruct you to give it a smart tug. Surely that is not too demeaning for you."

My temper had grown short, I confess, due to lack of rest, food, and the general tensions of the night. Conax pondered my remark, but said nothing, which was to the good. I do believe that a retort would have caused me to ignore his thews and paste him a stiff one in the mouth.

81

Gradually the breeze caught our much-patched sail. The little fishing boat began to race smartly toward open sea.

From my post at the stern, I watched the Island Kingdom drop behind us, splendid and imposing, its rooftops glinting in the first light. To see it so tranquil, one would hardly believe that within its walls disorder reigned, and supernatural beings stalked.

I was not an expert sailor by any means. But like all Atlanteans, I had enjoyed recreational boating as part of my upbringing. I managed to tack us quite far out, until we reached a spot where I deemed it safe to drop sail and anchor.

As soon as the lead ball plopped overside, I relaxed, hoping to catch a few winks. Unless my navigation erred, we lay far enough offshore so that we would be a mere blur to any watchers on the wall. I hoped we would be taken for fishermen trying different waters. Thus I also hoped to avoid the regular fishing fleet. When night descended, we would return to the beach and attempt to regain my villa.

I settled down to a sort of doze, but there was no real rest in it. My mind was haunted by spectral visions of the blue beings and their strange craft.

How had the apparition struck the ordinary, garden-variety Atlantean? Surely the craft's descent had been visible to any who were abroad.

Unless I missed my guess, the spectral sight would foment more fear and rumor. The citizens might well recall Babylos' warnings—and hold the corrupted government responsible for the bad omens.

I could not help a certain sly amusement. Geriasticus X, his debauched queen, and the entire grasping, pleasure-mad court had been guilty of so many crimes against the public good—both sins of commission and omission—that it was only a kind of ironic justice that they be held accountable for the heavenly visitations.

My dozing dreams did not improve. I saw Babylos gleefully proclaiming that damnation had arrived. I glimpsed Aphrodisia behind bars, alternately weeping and demanding instantaneous marriage.

But evidently I did fall into full slumber for a time, waking abruptly with the sun beating in my eyes.

The sky had cleared at last. The ocean sparkled. I heard a noisy splashing.

Sitting up, I spied Conax leaning over the gunwale. He gasped and cursed while his thews quivered briskly.

All at once, he brought his right hand out of the water. It

contained a large, wriggling fish of particularly oily appearance.

"Here," I yawned, "what are you doing?"

"Why, catching breakfast, naturally. My belly's as hollow as the cavernous caves of the noxious netherworld."

So saying, he sniffed the poor fish. One would have thought he inhaled perfumes from the East!

"Kindly throw that thing back in the water, Conax, or you shall lose your sailing master due to acute nausea."

"No stomach for a little raw fish? Why, many's the time I've chomped into an uncooked meal. There was the occasion when my cavalry and I caught some yak thieves, several of whom proved to be very tasty when——"

"Spare me!" I begged, gorge rising. "I have no palate for gourmet items."

"But surely you're hungry too! It's simple work to halve the fish——"

Again he held the sad looking specimen near his face. With a few gnashes of his teeth, he indicated how he proposed to divide it.

"Speak up, Hoptor! Do you want the head or tail?"

"N-n-neither," I replied, positioning my head over the rail and permitting nature to take its course.

I cannot offer a definitive statement as to whether he breakfasted on the fish. I was completely occupied elsewhere, thank the gods.

When I came upright again, he immediately commenced a rambling discourse on the effete ways of civilization, interspersed with laments for his lost broadsword, reiterations of his desire to return to his homeland, and promises that we Atlanteans would see how real men behaved, as soon as his reavers appeared to burn, loot, rape, torture, and murder. I perceived that unless I occupied myself, I would go mad listening to his monologue.

Therefore I restepped the mast, and proceeded to tack us further out to sea.

By this time, the Atlantean fisher-fleet had put out for the day. But only a fraction of the customary number of sails dotted the waves. Had further disorders disrupted the day's routine within the walls? We had no difficulty avoiding those few vessels which did sail out.

All day long we tacked up and down, up and down. By the time the sun's burning ball began to drop to the horizon, I had developed a sun-scald of painful proportions. All exposed parts of my body—but especially my cheeks and neck

—stung unmercifully. I could barely move without groaning.

Conax was still rambling on. Now it was something about disemboweling a warlock; evidently the fellow had taken a dislike to Conax's manners, and attempted to turn him into a shrub. Bleary with fatigue, hunger, and sunburn, I paid little attention.

"What's that you're mumbling?" Conax said. His eyes flashed in the glare of sunset. "Some snide comment about my tale?"

"I merely said that, within an hour, it will be dark. We can safely try beaching then."

"I am going to buy a new broadsword at the very first armor shop we encounter. By Crok, I intend to make someone pay for this humiliation. That a king of Chimeria should be forced to ride around all day in an open boat, without a single slave to work a fan—!"

As he continued his complaining, I stepped the mast for what I hoped would be the last time.

All the fisher-craft had returned to shore. The sunward side of fair Atlantis was bathed in the day's last red. I tugged on the anchor rope, hauled up the ball—fortunately my palms had escaped the blistering rays!—and through near super-human effort, got us started on a homeward course.

I was more irritable than ever, I don't mind confessing. I would be glad to be shed of the carping Chimerian, and have in his place more common folk, whom I could persuade to labor on my behalf!

The breeze promptly caught our sail, and started us back toward fair Atlantis, where the lamps of evening already gleamed.

We were clipping along through moderately heavy waves when suddenly, beneath the swells to port, twin spots of radiance appeared. I called Conax's attention to the double glow—eerie white, like a pair of huge eyes.

"Crok protect us, we're about to be attacked by a creature of the depths!"

So saying, he tore the mast from its socket!

The sail began to flap, the lines to fly and, abruptly robbed of its motive means, our tiny boat began to pitch wildly.

"Put back the sail, Conax! Do you want to capsize us?"

"I must have a weapon!" he insisted, gripping the mast at its midpoint while attempting to balance himself on wide-spread legs. I gripped the gunwale to prevent being hurled into the brine.

The twin radiances grew steadily brighter. They were very

near the surface now. In another moment, the sea monster appeared!

Foam poured off the spine-like upper fin. Water cascaded down between glowing exterior lanterns. I beheld a craft exactly like the one which had descended to Queen Voluptua's terrace!

Although transfixed with terror, I yet marveled at a machinery which could traverse air and water with equal facility.

Approximately a third of the craft became visible above the waves. As before, the patterned, metallic hull glowed. The craft moved neither forward nor backward, and I had the uncanny feeling that we were somehow being observed.

"Be very still, Conax," I whispered. "Perhaps the thing will go away."

"Are you making sport of me, Vintner? This is the same sea-dragon that appeared when my war vessel went down. I'll not miss a second chance to wreak vengeance."

And he threw back his head and began to utter his ululating battle-cry!

"No noise, Conax, for pity's sake! We've trouble enough alrea—*yowl!*"

His teeth closed smartly upon the hand with which I was trying to shut his mouth. A sudden tilt of the boat dumped me between the benches.

Conax, meantime, was merely warming up.

"Come out of that metal barrel and fight, you pusilanimous puppies of perdition! Come out, come out, I say! This is Conax the Chimerical challenging you!"

Silence greeted his shout; a scarifying stillness broken only by the murmur of wind and the lap of waves.

"What's the matter, you dogs? Why don't you answer me? I'll gain your attention some way! I mean to put you down, or make my death-stand doing it!"

"Oh, Conax, not your death-stand again—"

Would he heed? He would not. He raised the mast over his head. His thews rippled and twitched rapidly. He crouched down, then shot up by straightening his legs.

Propelled by the thrust, the mast sailed across the water. It struck the craft with a clang.

"Well, you've really done it now, Conax! Jump in the water and make your death-stand by yourself. I'm heading for Atlantis!"

Alas, I was too upset to carry out my promise efficiently. I dropped one oar into the water, and failed to set the second in place even after repeated tries.

The shining craft's upper spine, hinged at one side, fell over with a bang. A round portal was revealed; a different opening than the one from which the incline had descended on Voluptua's terrace.

At last I positioned my one oar. I began rowing furiously, only to realize that my effort turned us in a circle. Without warning, a blue being popped its head up through the hatch.

"We're discovered!" I cried, pulling madly on the oar. Such was my frantic state that I cared nothing for our drift or direction. I only wished to row as fast as possible.

My misplaced energy merely directed our little boat toward, not away from, the metallic craft. Disregarding Conax's boastful bellows, the blue being climbed out the hatch and stood on the hull. It was joined by a second blue personage, this one carrying what appeared to be a gold bell.

The blue being held the bell device upside-down. However, the bell did not ring. Instead, the blue one thrust its hand down into the bell opening. Whereupon, miraculous things took place.

Conax the Chimerical stiffened. His hands flew to his sides and remained there. From the wild antics of his thews, it was plain that he was gripped by some phantasmagorical force!

The first blue personage—what else might I call them? each bore two arms, a head, and two feet, unless more were concealed beneath their opulent robes—signed to the second, who performed additional manipulations within the depths of the bell device.

Without aid or support, Conax rose straight into the heavens, the distance of twice a man's height!

There he hovered, while his clenched teeth reflected the rays of the dying sun. I fell on my knees to importune the gods—this, surely, was my final moment!

Suddenly Conax sailed straight forward, wind blowing his hair helter-skelter. The blue beings stood away from the hatch as the barbarian came to a halt above it, suspended without wires or other visible apparatus!

Then he began to descend slowly, disappearing boots first through the opening.

"Greetings to you—and good-bye!" I called, falling on the oar again. I could not tell whether they understood me, but what had I to lose at the moment? "Your prisoner is a king of Chimeria, and he'll certainly fetch a fat ransom. I'm sure you're not interested in me, as I am but a lowly grower of grapes—"

Then—o dreadful fate!—the second blue being repeated

its manipulations within the bell. A tingling paralysis took possession of my body.

The oar dropped from my frozen hands. And I, like Conax, rose into the air!

At the apex of my ascent, I was drawn forward. Directly over the craft, I began to drop—straight toward the hole into which Conax had vanished.

I floated smoothly past the angular faces of the two blue personages. I recall glancing down between my sandals, to see what fate awaited.

I glimpsed several more blue faces peering up at me.

That is all I remember.

"Let me out, let me out!"

Thus my voice pealed for freedom, even before my eyes flew open.

I lurched up from a curious, spongy object which was evidently supposed to be a chair, but which returned to the contours of a colorful sphere when I left it. At once, the tingling force seized me. I was reseated gently but emphatically.

On my left hand, glowering Conax occupied a similar sphere-chair. He seemed restrained by invisible force, much as I was.

"Regrettably," said a mellifluous voice, "we cannot let you run around and let you interfere with the crew, since we are traveling beneath the liquid medium at a depth of eleventy-six—" at least that is what I believe I heard! —"frambs, and a speed of nine-plenty threepmores. Also, based upon physical studies conducted after you were brought aboard unconscious, it is our opinion that you would perish if you sought to escape into the liquid medium. Therefore, be comfortable. In order to prevent damage to this vessel, particularly on the part of your lively companion, we have been required to hold you with a force. As soon as you give evidence of being tractable, we shall unbind it. Then you will be free to move about."

The speaker, having moved around from behind me, turned out to be another of the blue personages. The garment it wore was nearly as peculiar as its features—a robe which seemed to radiate constantly changing light. How this was possible, I could not say, for the pebbly-textured garment bore no ornamentation whatsoever.

At close range, it became possible to detect individuality among the blue personages. Up to now, they had all seemed of identical visage. But who can blame me for such a prejudiced

87

judgment, given the circumstances under which I first encountered the creatures?

Our speaker, for example, was a bit more fully-fleshed in the cheeks, and possessed a longer jaw than some of his fellows. He confronted us in a circular, low-ceilinged chamber. Its continuous wall bore ever-shifting pastel patterns. Its floor resembled a seamless expanse of ivory, with hidden fires glowing beneath.

Then I grew conscious of a low, constant sound. The noise of magical machinery which drove the craft through the "liquid medium," perhaps? If so, it was machinery undreamed of by anyone I knew!

I would have been instantly reterrified, save for my sudden realization that I was, in fact, alive and breathing. I did not seem to be injured, either. Therefore, I addressed our host:

"I, Hoptor the Vintner, a fully enfranchised citizen of the Island Kingdom of Atlantis, demand that you release me at once."

"In return, do you pledge peacefulness and cooperation?"

"Of course!" At this juncture, I would have pledged anything.

The tingling sensation ceased. I was able to stand on my own unsteady legs.

The blue personage indicated Conax. "Can you offer the same guarantees for your companion?"

"Let me see."

I rushed over and whispered in Conax's ear, "If you know what's good for you, you won't attempt to injure this blue gentleman. Nor damage any of the furnishings. At least not until we learn the identity of these horrors. If you agree, that one will release you from the invisible bondage."

Conax grumped something about humiliation. But finally he gave a brusque nod. In a trice, he was on his feet.

Questions by the score overwhelmed my mind. The first one I uttered was, "We are truly beneath the sea?"

"If that is your term for the liquid medium, the answer is yes."

"Who are you, may I ask?"

"The ship's captain. It is I who will escort you to those who await."

"And who might they be? Atlanteans don't hobnob with just anyone, you know."

"The almighty ones," he returned. "Come."

"First tell us how you can converse in our language."

88

"On Zorop, we study every tongue. We are students of all the races of the stars."

"Zorop? I've never heard of an island called Zorop. Which direction does it lie?"

"That way," he said, pointing overhead, "a trillion-plenty"—at least I believe those were his words!—"fronks away. Zorop is not of this world."

✳ Ten ✳

I believe it is a fair statement—and no conceit!—to say that had Hoptor the Vintner not been accustomed to dealing with frequent changes of fortune, Hoptor the Vintner might have swooned dead away.

That I did not is proof that I am a man of courage and substance.

Also, from a practical standpoint, I was certainly no worse off among these blue personages, no matter what their devastating revelations, than I would have been in the presence of Pytho. At least, that was certainly the case up until the moment someone issued an execution order!

Therefore, I invited the captain of the craft to lead where he would.

We left the round chamber via a circular portal, proceeding through a sort of dim tunnel intersected on right and left by similar passageways. Various blue beings passed by, these dressed less opulently than our guide. They treated him deferentially, by means of a peculiar flexing motion of their digits.

Conax continued to scowl and mutter. I certainly hoped we'd honor his vow and check his temper. At least until we discovered how the land lay!

Ahead, I perceived another portal, curtained—if that's the term!—by an array of golden bubbles. Our guide emitted a bizarre whistling noise, and the bubbles all rushed to the portal's outer edges, leaving us free to pass through.

A sunken chamber lay beyond. But rather than conventional steps leading downward, I discovered another of those inclines.

Naturally I hesitated. Naturally Conax bumped me from behind.

Helpless, I stumbled onto the top of the incline. But rather than falling forward on my face, I remained upright. The incline itself seemed to grip my sandals, and I was conveyed smoothly to the bottom.

There, two blue beings were seated—if that's the word!—upon thin golden sticks rising from the floor. I marveled at the starkly functional design of this furniture.

The personage on the right was clad in a garment that glittered even more opulently than our guide's. His companion, of slighter build, wore a pebbly-textured robe emitting a softer glow. Though the facial structure of the two was basically the same, several tufts of blue hair grew from the head of the second. Each of these tufts was bound by a crystal ring. Had I at last encountered sex differentiation?

Searching for more obvious signs—chiefly bosoms—failed to yield an answer.

"All honor," intoned our guide. "We bring you two persons from yon island state. We plucked them from the liquid medium. The one of lesser height and greater girth calls himself Hop-tor the Vin-ner. I am unable to ascertain the meaning of the latter name."

"Vintner, vintner," I corrected. "It means a grower of wine grapes. My friend and I are of course happy to meet you folk, who obviously hail from a different country. Let us be the first to welcome—"

Rudely, Conax shouldered me aside.

"Don't confuse me with a cowardly, conniving Atlantean. I am a king of a mighty northern kingdom, and I'm not accustomed to being ordered about."

"King?" echoed the blue being I took for the male. The corners of his narrow mouth quirked. "We also! We must spend a gorf or two discussing how we both have been ill treated by the comrades of this one—"

And his thin blue digit indicated myself!

"If you mean you've been poorly received by the populace of Atlantis," I said, "as well as by the vested powers, it's no surprising. Affairs on the island are in a terrible state. I, for example, have been forced to flee for my life, unjustly accused of crimes of which I'm wholly innocent!"

Far be it from me to overlook an opportunity to get the point across! For even though I hadn't the vaguest idea about the origin of the blue persons, it was plain they were supreme in their limited sphere.

That sphere, at the moment, happened to be the depths of the sea, which I noted churning against a large window in the wall behind them. A large jellyfish floated up, studied the activity inside for a moment, and then, obviously bored, bobbled off to attack some chubby fish. I continued in my most helpful tone:

"Perhaps if you could give me some idea of the purpose of your visit, I could direct you to the proper authorities——"

"We have come," said the male, "to have congress with the native kind of this planet."

Wondering what a "planet" might be, I heard the female with the tufted hair say:

"Thus far, none has welcomed us with a dignity befitting our stations on distant Zorop."

"Exactly what are your stations on distant Zorop, if I may ask? Your captain employed the term almighty ones, and you, sir, made what I believe was a reference to kingship——"

"Yes," he said. "His Subservience used the correct honorific."

"His Subservience?" I repeated, wondering whether I'd heard aright.

"Chiefest of the chiefs of the many ships of our fleet," said the female. "Your host—Captain Mrf Qqt."

The captain flexed his digits at me!

At once I asked that his name be repeated. But even after several pronunciations, it remained—as far as I was concerned!—unpronounceable.

"And this," said the captain—beg pardon, His Subservience!—"this is His Splendor, Uulor Zrz. Next to him is Her Radiance, Mna Zra."

Conax snorted, "Idiotic names. They sound like the utterances of a steppe warrior with his mouth full of—oof!"

My elbow in the ribs quelled him just in time. I hastened to direct an apologetic smile at the monarchs.

I needn't have worried. They seemed unperturbed. But I wished to be sure.

"Believe me, Your Splendor and Your Radiance, we certainly appreciate being rescued from the oce—the liquid medium. As I tried to suggest, we were forced to take refuge in an open boat because of the unbridled vengefulness of a certain military officer in Atlantis——"

"At-lan-tis," echoed Uulor Zrz, the male. "That is the nearby island which we have unsuccessfully attempted to visit?"

"One hundred percent correct. Very good! But you must realize that you've been going at it the wrong way. Take your

91

vessels, now. Constantly whizzing back and forth in the heavens—those *are* your ships we've seen lately, am I right?"

"You are. Our exploration fleet is numerous. The other craft are, at the moment, in a patrol formation, there." He signed toward the sky.

"But when they're glimpsed by ordinary folk, their unusual radiance proves terrifying."

"Radiance is a function of astral travel," Mna Zra informed me.

"It does not attend our passage when the vessels sink beneath the liquid medium," noted His Splendor. "Only our way-lanterns shine then."

"Be that as it may, we Atlanteans aren't used to the sight of such fantastic machineries. Furthermore, when I encountered what I believe was one of your—ah—men—it happened at the imperial palace, during last night's storm—your representative failed to identify himself. And I was so taken by surprise, I believed the creat—ah, gentleman to be a demon."

"It is our procedure," said His Splendor, "to first pay a secret visit to any state with which we desire congress. To this end, we lower one or more of our officers by stealth, permitting them to observe conditions and report back. No doubt it was one such whom you encountered."

Then he fixed Conax with his immense, elongated eyes.

"Upon completion of the scouting of At-lan-tis, we made our decision to land and give greetings. This we did. Our memory reminds us that we were harried by our fellow king."

He didn't seem overly upset. But he was putting us on the spot, all the same. To his mate he added:

"You, sweet consort, happily failed to witness the unfriendly exchange."

Before I could even begin to explain, Conax assumed a menacing posture.

"So you were one of the thrice-cursed curs who humiliated the ruler of Chimeria!"

"There was no intent of humiliation. We merely decided, based upon what happened, that unfavorable confluences of the starry portents must have precluded a warm welcome just then. In order not to impair relations at a more favorable time later, we made ourselves rid of you in the gentlest possible manner, and departed."

Bright blue lids dropped briefly over his queer eyes, then disappeared up in his skull again. My spine chilled a little, because His Splendor's tone had become a mite less cordial.

"Had we desired, O king, we could have easily dealt with you in a manner befitting your rudeness."

"That," Conax shrieked, "I don't believe for one minute! Get off that stick and fight like a human being! Fight, I say, you—"

His Subservience reached out and tapped Conax on the head, gently. The barbarian sprawled in a semi-daze.

His Splendor said, "That is but a sampling. Half-strength. Kindly behave."

Her Radiance tugged at her blue hair as if piqued.

"Does your companion always act so rashly?"

"No, no, it's merely a nervous reaction. True, he's a powerful king. But he doesn't know much about civilized ways."

Conax had clambered to his feet. He appeared to be casting about for furniture to smash. The captain, His Subservience, extended his hand, ready to provide another cranial tap. Conax cooled down at once.

Her Radiance uttered a disconsolate sigh.

"Everywhere we travel upon this planet, the reception is the same. Resistance, rejection, shrill outcries of terror—we come in peace and we are treated as foes!"

"Well, as I have tried to suggest, you get a hot reception in part because your appearance is so—ah—unusual. It's quite a jolt to all but the most sophisticated. You have said you hail from a place called Zorop—"

"Another planet!" exclaimed His Splendor. "Another world! Lying an immense distance across space—"

"Do you mean to tell me that Zorop is not on this same piece of terra firma which holds the Inland Seas, the Misty Outer Kingdoms, the Pillars, stinking Lemuria and fair Atlantis? Come, I heard your captain claim something like that. But I hardly believed him! The notion's ridiculous. As everyone knows, the world is shaped like a dinner plate. It's round and flat, and kingdoms and oceans repose on its upper surface. It is completely surrounded by a crystalline envelope in which the heavenly lights twinkle. Since there is nothing but featureless void beyond the envelope, I simply can't accept your statement that you come from another 'planet.' No offense intended, of course!"

Whereupon, in the space of minutes, I received a lesson in cosmology that struck me dumb with wonder.

These Zorophim—that being the inclusive term for all blue beings—insisted that fair Atlantis was merely one dot upon a large ball of matter whirling in "space"—and that no solid envelope whatsoever surrounded the ball!

They maintained that eight or nine similar balls of matter —all lifeless!—were located within a reasonable distance of ours. All the balls, they said, traveled in fixed patterns, in relationship to the sun.

"No, no!" I disputed. "The sun—the Eye of Heaven—is affixed to the inside of the envelope. It slides from one end of the envelope to the other, then back again, bringing day to some locations on the dinner plate, while night claims the others."

Gently, as if tutoring an infant, His Splendor stated that this was not the case at all. He said "space" was open—uncircumscribed!—and that beyond our own relatively small neighborhood of balls, there were countless other balls and suns quite some number of "fronks" away. The "planet" Zorop was one such ball, whirling around its own far-off sun.

"Enough, stop!" I cried, pressing my throbbing temples. "It's more than even my educated mind can grasp!"

"But we have tried to explain clearly and simply—"

"Surely it can't be true! Surely you've come from some other kingdom affixed to the remote edge of the great dinner plate—!"

"Superstition and ignorance!" sighed His Splendor, rising from the golden stick and pacing to the window. "It is everywhere upon this benighted sphere. Of course Zorop is not of this planet! Have you ever seen crafts such as this one before?"

"You've got a point there," I admitted, hoping to soothe his irritation. "On the other hand, you must realize that all this talk of balls and suns and vast distances measured in 'fronks' simply contradicts my entire upbringing. If you indeed belong to a superior race from far away, why trouble yourselves visiting our dinner pla—uh, planet, where you have received nothing but insults? Had you named myself to be your emissary at the court of Atlantis, I might interpolate, your reception could have been entirely different!"

A hit! His Splendor turned back from the window. Even Her Radiance looked interested.

"You are well-known to those who hold power on the walled island?"

"Oh, yes, I'm very well-known. A mention of the name Hoptor brings all sorts of immediate attention."

"Then perhaps," mused His Splendor, "this is a well-met moment. You ask why the Zorophim take wing. Leave the comforts of their idyllic home planet—voyage a trillion-plenty fronks through space—explore world after world in search of intelligent life. It is because, unless the current trend is reversed, Zorop perishes."

"Well, I'd call that good riddance," commented Conax.

I elbowed him.

"If you do that once more, you toadying, overstuffed—"

His Subservience, Captain Mrf Qqt, raised a potent hand. Conax bit his lips and fell silent. But his eyes promised hot-tempered vengeance at a later time.

I asked His Splendor why Zorop was facing doom. He answered:

"It is a matter of the Sacred Fuel."

"Sacred Fuel? What might that be?"

Pleased by my feigned interest, he replied, "Since you seem more reasonable than your companion—indeed, you are the first even-dispositioned inhabitant of your world we have encountered!—allow me to show, rather than tell."

And so saying, he led the way up the incline.

Her Radiance went with us. But Conax, who immediately commenced complaining, was tapped on the head and rendered prone. I hoped the rest might make him more temperate.

From the passage which I had traversed before, we turned to the right, into a similar way. Shortly, His Splendor signed to the left.

Once more we descended an incline—this rather longer; I was beginning to get the hang of it!—to a sort of gallery overlooking a large chamber where blue beings scurried in and out among half a dozen round, open vats. The vats brimmed with a dark purplish liquid, which was apparently pumped out through a complex network of transparent pipes.

All attending the vats flexed their digits out of respect for the royal presence. Then they continued in their incomprehensible chores. The king said:

"Below, you see the Sacred Fuel. It is the wellspring—the source—of civilization on Zorop. This craft is powered by it. All our ubflabs are illumined by it"— (I declined to ask the nature of an ubflab. A public structure, might it be?) —"indeed, all of Zorophimian culture is centrally rooted in the supply of Sacred Fuel. In our world's dim beginnings, there was an abundance. But ours is a very ancient planet, growing more populous with each passing zapz. Due to these increased demands, as well as to certain temporary climatological setbacks, the supply of Sacred Fuel is running dangerously low. In a few more whambs, all will be gone—and life as we know it on Zorop will expire."

Wonderstruck, I asked, "And there is no means by which you can create additional quantities?"

"None," said Her Radiance. "Our finest minds have studied the problem. They have exhausted every known possibility."

"Thus," continued her consort, "equipped with our knowledge of the inhabited planets—there are quite a few of those, you know—we have visited each in turn, searching for wellsprings of the Sacred Fuel. We intend to locate a supply which will enable Zorop to flourish for another plenty-thousand lubs or more."

"How has your search fared so far?"

"We have been away from our home world an aumox already. And each stop has been more disappointing than the last. Nowhere can we find the Sacred Fuel. Oh, there's life aplenty—and usually it's hostile, just as here. So we leave—without Sacred Fuel."

"But if you fail to find it anywhere—!" I exclaimed.

"Extinction," he intoned. "The darkness. The end."

"Whew," I said, "that's a heartrending tale."

Once more I glanced down at the vats; the mysterious purple liquid was fuming and foaming.

"I'm sorry to say, Your Splendor, that offhand I don't know of any supply either. Perhaps if you indicated its composition—?"

Her Radiance poured out a string of terms, until at last I raised my hand.

"It's no use, I can't understand. Is it possible to translate that gibber—uh, formula?"

"According to our linguistic studies, there are no equivalents," His Splendor answered. His shoulders seemed to fall, despairingly. "Perhaps the search is futile, as we are beginning to suspect. Come, we are weary of this place—"

I followed the king and queen up the incline, and back to the audience chamber, where I now saw an opening in the ceiling. Through it, I perceived the moon, luminous behind stormy clouds. The craft had surfaced, though how and when His Splendor had issued the order remained a mystery.

"Let us arise for a breath of fresh blope," said His Splendor, stepping under the opening and immediately levitating.

I followed suit, intrigued to find myself likewise lifted.

With agile movements, His Splendor negotiated the roll of the craft, holding fast to the ornamental spine. I did likewise. Her Radiance had opted not to join us.

Thus, in company with the monarch of distant Zorop—if I could believe in such a "planet!"—I clung to the fantastical ship and looked longingly at lamplit Atlantis rising from the night-dark sea.

That sea, I might mention, had grown quite choppy. The clouds scudding before the moon looked distinctly menacing. Another storm on the way; one awful omen after another!

"That is your homeland, then, Hoptor?"

"Fair Atlantis," I nodded, not without a sentimental tremor.

"A cruel, unattractive place. Though a cut above one or two others we have visited. None can compare with Zorop. Ah, Zorop, Zorop! Shall our eyes behold you ever again? Shall we once more revel in your justice? Your learning, your culture, your intrapersonal harmony? Aye, perhaps not—!"

A moment of silence; then a sharp gesture.

"But this melancholy ill befits a monarch! We must turn our thoughts to more practical matters. Since your state, too, evidently knows nothing of the Sacred Fuel, further visitation is fruitless. Therefore, in return for what has been a generally agreeable visit—once we calmed your furious companion!—we shall immediately order this craft to fly you home."

O nausea! And not from the rolling sea, either.

"But Your Splendor—I don't dare go back—that is, I don't wish to go back—that is, I couldn't possibly trouble you—"

"Nonsense," he replied, "it's no trouble. We shall depart at once."

✳ Eleven ✳

Imagine my dismay at this turn of events!

Having behaved agreeably in the presence of the curious Zorophim, I was about to be repaid by a kindness which would do nothing short of plunge me back into danger. Happily, in such a plight, my native wit didn't desert me.

I had no sooner followed His Splendor down to the circular room, via the now-familiar levitation process, than I made so bold as to say:

"Before we do anything hasty, let's discuss the subject of

the Sacred Fuel again. If I were to be appointed, let's say, Official Liaison Officer of the Zorophim to the Court of His Exaltedness, Geriasticus X—why, by virtue of my many connections and acquaintances, I might be able to reward your search."

The blue ruler countered, "But did you not state that you lacked any knowledge of Sacred Fuel sources?"

"True, true! But I was speaking personally—and I'm only a simple vintner. It would behoove you to converse with some of our many savants—" (Frankly, I couldn't name a single one, save addled Babylos; but sometimes truth must be adjusted to suit a higher purpose!) "They might possess the information I lack."

Hope gleamed in those elongated eyes. "Do you really think so, Vintner?"

"Oh, very definitely—provided you permit me to establish you at court, via the proper procedures and protocols—"

The discussion continued for some additional time. Even I blush to recall the many outrageous misstatements I was required to make in order to convince him. Suffice it to say, the quest of the Zorophim was of such great importance that he finally agreed.

As a direct consequence, I was soon ferried within wading distance of the beach.

The Zorophim could extinguish their craft's exterior lanterns at will. Thus we approached the shore undetected. His Subservience, Captain Mrf Qqt, was going to come along, a circumstance I wasn't too happy about. But His Splendor insisted.

Mrf Qqt affixed a silver disc to his forehead by means of a chain which he slipped round his skull. This, I was told, would enable him to communicate instantly with his superiors, informing them as soon as I had arranged a court audience.

Therefore, I gathered up my now-begrimed cloak and slid down the side of the craft into the surf, landing navel-deep but upright. Conax followed suit, grumbling over not being kept informed about what was happening.

The captain was more agreeable, content to follow my lead and slog to shore without comment. We landed near the point where we had embarked—in another age, it seemed. Many wondrous events had transpired in the interim, as I was reminded when the vessel of the Zorophim rose straight up from the foam, torrents of water draining down its sides. Higher and higher it climbed. Now nothing could conceal its iridescent glow.

98

At a suitable altitude, it flashed away horizontally, to rendezvous somewhere behind the clouds with its sister ships.

"Come on," I told the others wearily. "Up the wall and down again. And look sharp for soldiers."

Fair Atlantis had quieted during our absence. At least I did not detect the presence of armed might on every corner. The night had grown ominously dark, the clouds hiding the moon once more. Lightning began to flicker intermittently.

Perhaps it was my fatigue, but I wondered if all this hustling and scheming would ultimately prove to be for naught. Perhaps gods greater than either I or the Zorophim could imagine were preparing an unhappy fate for us all.

Rotten Row, at least, seemed its old self. A member of the gentry was being throttled in the shadows near the Bloody Bench. I thought I recognized a friendly face.

"Ho, Mimmo, you scalawag. Tear yourself away long enough to do me a favor."

Recognizing me at once, he left the gentleman struggling in the grip of his five- and six-year-old assistants. I had asked His Subservience to stand well back in the dark, and he had earlier donned a cloak which did not shimmer. But there was simply no concealing the glint of the disc chained to his forehead. It immediately attracted Mimmo's greedy eye.

I boxed Mimmo's ears.

"You little rascal, can't you recognize cheap goods? The man's a traveling necromancer—a worker of marketplace stunts."

"Oh yes? Is that why his dial's all blue?"

"Hasn't had time to remove his makeup. Gave a whole series of performances tonight. Now pay attention, and I'll reward you handsomely later. Go into the Bloody Bench. See if there's anyone present who is trustworthy. If so, fetch him."

Mimmo nodded and hopped off, though not before he fixed us with a piercing glance I did not understand.

Shortly he returned with aged Rheumus, an acquaintance of long standing. I had helped Rheumus obtain pension payments by testifying that he was lame. In fact, he was spry as a cat. Mimmo shot off down the street at top speed, while I inquired about the general situation.

"Very bad, Hoptor," Rheumus coughed. He was forever feigning infirmities in order to beg zebs. "Right after you dropped out of sight, General Pytho's men rounded up a flock of so-called undesirables. Many were executed, hundreds more thrown in prison—"

"In heaven's name, what's the reason for such injustice?"

"Them lights that's been flashing has got everybody saying Atlantis is accursed. Most folk think a cataclysm's due—"

A well-timed ruffle of thunder punctuated his remarks dramatically!

"—and them that's still at liberty are furious with old ivory-mouth. There's either ruin or rebellion brewing. Maybe both."

"Thanks for the counsel, Rheumus. I'm off for my villa—"

"Ssh! Don't say that so loud! You obviously don't know what else has happened."

"Tell me!"

"The general's put a price on your head. A whopper. Two hundred and fifty zebs. Why, if you'n me didn't have a history of friendship, I might be tempted myself— Say, who's your friend with the jewelry on his head?"

But I was already departing the scene, cursing General Pytho's vindictiveness.

Fortunately, we were able to reach my house undetected. All the soldiers had been withdrawn, probably on the theory that I would not be foolish enough to return. Perhaps our return was rash. But we needed a base of operations.

We scaled the wall, passed through the garden, and proceeded to my study. With stylus and tablets, I immediately drafted a message:

> MEMORANDUM:
> From: the Official Liaison Officer of the Zorophim.
> To: His Exaltedness, Geriasticus X.
> Subj: Marvelous royal beings from another "planet,"
>   intercourse with.

Thereafter, in a succession of well-chosen phrases, I sketched the arrival of the blue monarchs, briefly noted the many marvels I'd witnessed as their guest, and mentioned the desire of the Zorophim to meet with Geriasticus under conditions more pleasant than they had encountered earlier.

Further, I advised that the visitors be received with extreme courtesy and high honor, as their vessels were the source of the heavenly lights. Once their presence was explained to the populace, I stated, panic would disappear, and Geriasticus X would zoom up to his former heights of popularity.

On the final tablet, I outlined my terms for helping to bring about a mutually advantageous audience. Those terms, of course, included full pardon for myself.

I then signed *Hoptor the Vintner*, underneath repeating my title, just to make certain.

100

When I had read portions of my memorandum aloud, Conax said, "But how do we deliver that to the palace?"

"Why, you shall take it. It's time you held up your end again. In one of the portions I didn't read, I asked for your pardon along with that of several others. See for yourself—"

I displayed the tablets, which I doubted he could read. In point of fact, I had, in my haste, neglected to mention his name.

"Umm, yes, I see," he said, which only proves the conceit of kings!

"Only you, Conax, have the sheer force of personality to persuade the palace guards to let you speak to Geriasticus. I'll provide what support I can. Follow me."

In a rear room, I located a poor-quality sword I had once purchased when the neighborhood was undergoing a rash of burglaries. The flimsy weapon seemed to restore Conax's confidence. He departed through the front doors, slashing the air and making barking noises, the tablets tucked beneath his other arm.

While Mrf Qqt amused himself by wandering through my villa to peer and poke at the unfamiliar furnishings, I set about drafting a set of tablets identical with the first. In truth, I was not at all certain that Conax would come through alive. In the event that he didn't—alarming thought!—I would have to go myself.

At least two hours went by. Then, between claps of thunder, I heard a groan from the garden.

I flung aside the study hangings, rushed down the hall, and thence outdoors. Conax had just dropped over the wall. He was a veritable patchwork of sword cuts!

"Conax, what happened to you?"

"I encountered quarrelsome guards." All at once, he grinned. "They tasted iron, to their everlasting regret."

"Didn't you manage to talk your way into the king's presence?"

"No, unfortunately, I lost my temper before—"

"You rash rogue, you've ruined everything!"

"In what way? I didn't talk my way to Geriasticus, I fought my way. Maiming at least a dozen of his toadies en route! I hewed a bloody path straight to the old fool's sleeping rooms, and surprised him in his nightgown, with his ivory mouthpieces lying nearby. Of course, by then, a pack of baying hellhounds pursued me. By thrusting the tablets into the king's hands, then holding the doors shut with nothing save the strength of my thews, I gave him time to read all that babble

101

you wrote. At first he looked as though he'd glimpsed the abyss. Then he questioned me—all the while my pursuers were beating the door with a battering ram. But the thews of Conax held fast! When I vouched for the presence of the Zorops or whatever you call them, the king instantly brightened up. I've never seen such a swift change, in fact. He read me that passage about his popularity, seizing it as a rat a cheese. He bade me admit the soldiers—they fell on their arses when I removed myself suddenly—and he forbade them to touch so much as a hair of my head. Then he ordered me to return here, and bid you arrange a formal visit by the Zorops. Oh, yes. He also granted your terms. Aphrodisia and that soothsayer will be freed at first light. Here, it's all written on this little tablet and marked with his seal. In sum, not a bad night's work!"

So saying, he flexed his blood-stained biceps proudly.

"Well, Your Subservience," I said to Mrf Qqt, who had joined us, "we have won a small victory from Geriasticus at last. Principally because he needs to restore the people's faith and calm their fears. We must immediately communicate with your—"

Knocking resounded within the house.

"I hope that's not soldiers," I said. "Conax, where is your sword?"

"Stuck in some lieutenant's leg, I believe."

"Then I must prepare other defenses!" I rushed toward the house, urging him to follow.

"No, thanks, I've done my share," he replied, dogging me into my study. He picked up a flagon of wine and, humming, began to empty it over his wounds.

Seizing the heaviest taboret available, I pressed Mrf Qqt into following me to the street doors, where the knocking was repeated, louder this time.

"You turn this handle, Captain. Then step back. I, crouching to one side with the taboret raised, will dispatch whoever has come to arrest us."

Nodding, he released the latch. A gray oblong appeared on the floor—it was indeed the first crack of morning. A voice exclaimed, "Praise be, we're free—!"

I brained the entrant as he entered, discovering his identity as he fell.

"Babylos! And Aphrodisia! My little vintage—! *Argh!* Why are you hitting me that way?"

"Why did you hit *him?*" she returned.

"I, I—" Dodging her fists, I attempted to explain: "

thought it might be soldiers, trying to collect the reward on my head. An honest error—gods! Will you kindly stop that?"

"I don't know when I've ever met such a vexatious person!" she exclaimed, delivering one final blow to my ribs.

"How have I vexed you, Aphrodisia? I told you that striking Babylos was an accident!"

"You've vexed me by not honoring your promises of marriage! Had we been husband and wife, none of this would have happened!"

"Aphrodisia, I find it inconceivable that you can think of marriage at a time like this. Events of unparalleled significance are taking place, but you utterly fail to appreciate—"

Just then, Babylos woke with a groan. He sat up, spied Mrf Qqt, shrieked and fainted.

Aphrodisia turned to look. She likewise shrieked and fainted.

Now I was the one who was sorely vexed! Mrf Qqt helped me drag Babylos to the study. I seized the wine jar from Conax —by now his wounds reeked like a dozen taverns!—and emptied what remained over the old soothsayer's head.

Babylos stirred, and licked his lips. Then he commenced raving about grape-flavored rain, another sure sign of the doom of Atlantis. I left the study forthwith, carrying Aphrodisia outside for some reviving fresh air.

Fresh air indeed! The wind blew through the garden at near gale force. The heavens were an unrelieved panorama of gray, lit frequently by garish lightning. The storm would be a notable one when at last it broke.

I sat on a bench and chafed Aphrodisia's wrists, unaccountably touched by her bedraggled beauty. I certainly didn't plan to let her know how I felt, though! Affecting a stern expression, I began to tweak her cheeks.

"Come dear, let's stop this gasping and fainting. Wake up, that's a good girl—weighty matters of state await us!"

Her sparkling blue eyes flew open.

"Hoptor! Was that a devil I saw? Are we dead and already in hell?"

"Naturally not! Don't you recognize my garden?"

"But who—or *what*—?"

In my gentlest tone, I said, "Calm yourself, Aphrodisia. I am fully in control of the situation. There isn't time for me to explain everything. But here's a bit of it. That devil's no devil, but one of the Zorophim, inhabitants of a distant sphere, or 'planet,' as they call them. He may be alarming at first glance. But he's a perfectly polite, not to say civilized, fellow.

Indeed, once you get over the fact that he's blue, you'll find he's a thoroughly fine chap. I have arranged a high level meeting between his king and Geriasticus X—never mind how, that would take an hour to tell. But with matters of statecraft on my mind, I must ask that you shift for yourself for a time—"

Unwise words! She flung her arms about my neck.

"I am abandoned in a dungeon, then freed for but an hour, and you tell me I must shift for myself. I will not, Hoptor. Not until I have received a definitive and long overdue answer as to when you plan to marry me. Blue persons—statecraft—I don't care a zeb for those! I demand to know, once and for all—"

"Oh, a pretty domestic scene!"

The sudden squeal galvanized me to attention, and caused Aphrodisia to—what else?—faint.

"Captain Num!" I cried, dumbfounded, even as he rushed into the garden. He was accompanied by half a dozen fully-armed soldiers.

I became aware of sounds of struggle within the house. I cursed myself roundly for neglecting to latch the front doors.

"I insist on knowing the meaning of this intrusion!"

"The meaning?" he jeered. "Why, it takes no seer to fathom that. You're under arrest."

"Arrest? You err! I have been granted the protection of Geriasticus X."

"I know nothing about that. I do know about the substantial reward for your apprehension. I plan to divide it with my dear little informant, there—"

I turned. And who did I see watching from atop the garden wall? Mimmo!

The depraved child had the nerve to say, "Sorry to turn you in, sir. But my sister needs an operation."

"Captain Num, you are making a calamitous mistake. You had better consult with your sweet—uh, the general, before you move against me. I have been appointed Official Liaison Officer—"

"Don't try to confuse me with your slick chatter, Hoptor. You have eluded punishment and embarrassed General Pytho once too often."

So saying, he brandished his sword and cried, "Attack!"

✳ Twelve ✳

Captain Num lunged forward. I leaped aside and stuck out my foot. He spilled heels over helmet. With his nose buried among my vines, he squealed for assistance.

But the half dozen soldiers were busy cringing at the sight of His Subservience, who had appeared in the doorway behind them. I, meantime, was attempting to conceal myself among the grapes.

Not in order to avoid conflict. No indeed, that is a false accusation! I wished to locate a weapon. That I was crawling toward the wall, rather than toward the door to my villa, was just a part of my plan to elude detection.

With Aphrodisia fainted, and Captain Num and I thrashing amidst the grapes, poor Mrf Qqt seemed at a loss about what to do. Two soldiers started toward him hesitantly. His Subservience was clever enough to deduce that, since the soldiers were pointing swords at him, they must be unfriendly. As his arms were longer than the military blades, it was a simple matter for him to reach out and tap the nearest man aside the helmet.

Exactly as Conax had done, the soldier collapsed, unconscious. The other would-be stabber retreated at once.

Mrf Qqt wore a quizzical expression, as if, being of mighty intellect, he could not comprehend such physical goings-on. For my part, I continued my strategic maneuver toward the wall.

A few drops of rain spattered my neck. The wind blew harder now, and thunder rumbled steadily.

"Look, you dunderheads!" cried Captain Num. "That fat wander is escaping—stop him!"

I was not in a frenzy of fear, as has been maintained. No, I had simply decided that it would be too difficult to gain the villa by circling the garden. I intended to reenter by the front door. And it was for this reason that I was attempting to scale the wall!

Ah, unhappy Hoptor, who permitted himself to become

105

freighted with extra flesh! Though scaling the wall was not impossible when I was in a less heated state of mind, somehow, in the terror of this moment, I could not do it. On the third try, my fingers came within an ace of catching hold of the top. But I lost my grip and tumbled back into the grapes.

Behind, I heard the crash of boots damaging the vines. Twisting my head, I perceived Num leading two soldiers toward me rapidly. I hurled the nearest available weapon—a cluster of half-ripened grapes.

That failed to do much good. So there I was, pinned against the wall, with a trio of assassins rushing me full speed. It certainly looked like the end for Hoptor the Vintner! I once again regretted not being more religious.

This sudden attack of moralism proved unnecessary, however. Captain Num and the soldiers were checked at the last moment by an ululating war-cry from the far side of the garden.

Conax's forehead was bloodied. His pelt-cloak was rent in many places. Bits of my furniture clung to his hair and shoulders. But a sword glinted in his upraised hand!

His thews quivered at an unprecedented rate. He gripped his sword hilt with both hands, and, chanting vengeful appeals to Crok, advanced into the fray, hewing the air all about him.

"Berserker, berserker!" shrieked one soldier, instantly dropping his sword to flee.

Let me draw a partial veil across the next few moments. Tender sensibilities would reel at a description of the carnage.

Sufficient to say, once Conax the Chimerical got hold of a sword, our troubles were temporarily over.

Severed limbs threw through the air willy-nilly. Captain Num, that depraved dandy, was no match for a mighty barbarian. Soon Conax was tossing Num's head up and down like a ball.

"Care for a little trophy of the engagement, Hoptor?"

That proved a bit too grisly even for my blasé nature. I fainted.

Eventually, of course, I awoke; Conax assisted me by cuffing my face so hard I thought my head would fly off.

Temporarily sated, his entire person gore-bespattered, he was more pleasant than I had ever seen him. He even apologized gruffly, for he thought he had been stinging my cheek with light blows.

"Light blows to you, perhaps. But enough to addle my brain for life. Try to remember I'm not one of the enemy."

"Easily done, since, in battle-born bloodlust, I dispatched

every last one. Too bad there weren't more," he pouted, "I was just getting warmed up."

He poked his sword into a nearby corpse a few times. "Alas!" he sighed, "utterly defunct."

Before my gorge could rise further, I signed to Mrf Qqt. "Quick, we must hide the evidence!"

With the aid of the captain from Zorop and a reluctant Conax, I performed the disagreeable task of removing the dead to the wine cellar, both portions of Captain Num included. I took a brace of large jars back upstairs with me, opening these for my guests.

I tried to remain indifferent to the damage done to my furnishings. In truth, it looked as if Conax had managed to wreck every last item of worth.

However, larger matters pressed.

I was concerned about little Mimmo; he had disappeared during the fray. Would he report us to someone else? I had no way of telling.

I poured some wine down Aphrodisia's throat. When both she and Babylos had recovered, I begged their indulgence and, swiftly, explained the presence and origin of Mrf Qqt. I also touched on the circumstances leading to our return to my villa.

Naturally there were outpourings of disbelief and wonder. But being an essentially pleasant individual, Mrf Qqt soon calmed the worst of their apprehensions. I am happy to report that my revelations were of such a staggering nature that Aphrodisia quite forgot to mention more about marriage.

Rather, she inquired, "What becomes of us now?"

"As far as I can see," I said, "there is but one course open. This house is not safe, especially with that greedy Mimmo at large. We must remove ourselves to the palace immediately."

"Exactly what I wanted to hear!" exclaimed Conax. "The gory gobbets in the garden were mere morsels—red appetizers for a bloody banquet to come—"

And, throwing his head back, he began to bark.

"Will you calm yourself?" I cried. "There'll be no more battles today!"

"What? We're not going to storm the corruption-wracked walls of that palace of perdition?"

"We certainly are not. We are going to enter peaceably, by the main gate, and immediately place ourselves under the protection of Geriasticus X."

Mrf Qqt said, "That would seem a prudent course. Has

not the lord of your Island Kingdom agreed to the terms offered by you, as Official Liaison Officer?"

"He has."

"Thus, in order to arrange a congress between my rulers and yours, we must speak with the king Geriasticus in person. Let us away at once!"

"Marvel of marvels!" crooned Babylos. "It will be a congress of universal historical importance! And I shall be privileged to write the official account!"

"Don't be too sure," Aphrodisia countered. "Are you positive we can trust that old fool, Hoptor?"

"Geriasticus? Did he not fling open your prison cell? Did he not grant my demands in full?"

"Yes, I suppose he did, but—"

"Don't plague me with quibbles, Aphrodisia. The longer we wait to throw ourselves on his mercy, the longer we risk the less tender mercies of his underlings."

She fully understood my reference to Pytho, and this stilled her opposition.

Since my splendid house was virtually a total shambles, I saw no need to lock it up. I secured a clean cloak for myself, and one for Aphrodisia. After making certain I had the little tablet bearing the seal of Geriasticus, we set out for the palace with all speed.

Conax had refused the offer of a spare garment, preferring to let the raindrops wash the gore from his thews. He marched along humming a martial air; I had never seen him in such a jolly temper.

The day had grown dark as midnight. Only ragged patches of white sky showed between swift-flying black clouds. Of a sudden, Babylos pointed upward. We saw a formation of light discs on the wing.

"Merely a portion of our fleet on patrol," His Subservience assured us. When I inquired about the exact size of the armada of exploration, he informed me that it numbered "eighty-many whonkles." Satisfied that the craft were numerous, I let it go at that.

Unfortunately the rest of the populace, not being on intimate terms with the Zorophim, still took a dim view of the flying lights, as we discovered crossing an avenue not far from the palace.

"Look, Hoptor," Aphrodisia said. "Is that a parade down there in the next block?"

I studied the crowd, including the clubs and firebrands.

"No, I believe it's a civil disorder. The citizens are doubtless

108

engaged in rioting and looting because they've become convinced there's no tomorrow. Our presence at the palace will help change that situation!"

Propelled by these new civic considerations, we rushed onward. We saw two similar outbreaks in progress before we reached the main gate of the palace.

I presented myself at the guard booth and flourished the king's tablet.

"We wish immediate audience with His Exaltedness. And he with us. Here, you'll note his message as proof of what I say."

The dolt peered at the tablet. "Can't read a word of it. I was forced to quit barracks school when I failed the examination on siege engine operation."

"Come, come, I don't want to hear your personal history. Surely you recognize your ruler's seal!"

"Yes, I recognize that much. However," he added, strangely glum, "if you wish an audience with His Exaltedness, now you'll have to ascend to the sacred skies. Or perhaps descend to the sizzling fires, if one can believe the stories about him."

"What kind of nonsense are you speaking, man?"

He pointed across the courtyard fronting the main wing of the palace. I perceived figures marching through a colonnade.

Tapers glowed. Mallets thumped a slow beat on drumheads.

"A festival day? I don't recall—"

"Listen more closely," Aphrodisia whispered. "There is wailing—lamentation—"

I peered through the drizzle as the procession began to cross the court toward the temple. Gods! Priests swinging censers led the way. And those who followed all wore black.

Then I spied Swinnia, and Lady Voluptua, both tearing their garments and their hair.

Eight eunuchs appeared from the colonnade, bearing an ornate bier on their shoulders. Other eunuchs shielded the bier with a canopy on poles. On the bier reposed a figure swathed to its chin in robes of state. There was no mistaking the flash of ivory between the stiff jaws.

"His Exaltedness is deceased?" I gasped.

"Yes," said the man on guard. "A sudden attack of the flux. Happily, he was not alone when it happened. General Pytho was at his side, discussing matters of state. Before His Exaltedness winged his way to heaven—or wherever it is he went—he laid his hand on the general's shoulder. He named him heir to the kingdom."

"But how do you know that?" Aphrodisia exclaimed.

"General Pytho informed the palace at a special formation soon after the unhappy moment. Oh, you should have seen the general's tears."

Tears of joy, I wagered! At long last, Pytho's lustful ambitions had borne fruit.

"While the general wept," the soldier continued, "he assured us there would be continuity of rule. Following the memorial service in the temple"— a gesture toward the procession—"the high priests will administer the oath of office. So if you wish an audience with His Exaltedness, Pytho I, you'll probably have to wait awhile in his chambers."

Aphrodisia sensed the potential peril.

"Perhaps we shouldn't risk it, Hoptor—"

I was busy pondering the alternatives. The new king was certainly no friend—especially now that Conax had dispatched his paramour! But Pytho needn't know that. I for one did not intend to play the blabbermouth!

Further, we still had a certain bargaining power. Though a vile villain, Pytho was no fool. Like Geriasticus X, he would—I hoped!—see the wisdom of using the Zorophim to explain the many recent bad omens. Thus he might still the public's fear, which was even now being manifested in the riotous sprees we'd witnessed.

I did not like the route which lay ahead. But I liked its alternatives even less.

Accordingly, I informed the soldier that we would await Pytho I in his chambers.

"Very well, pass on."

"Thank you."

"Don't mention—say, aren't you the vintner called Hoptor? I thought there was something familiar about you."

"Why do you wish to know?"

He commented that there were several warrants extant for my apprehension and arrest.

"Well, His Exaltedness Pytho I will soon set those aside!" I replied. "If that were not the case, do you imagine I would show up here in person?"

That confounded him utterly, giving us time to hurry ahead through the rain.

"I didn't know Geriasticus had caught the flux," Aphrodisia commented.

"Are you serious? I expect he caught it, to use your term, from poisoned wine or a knife wielded in stealth. Pytho was alone with him when he expired, remember."

We swung to the left, around the courtyard wall, wishing to avoid the last of the funeral procession. But we encountered sime difficulty reaching General Pytho's quarters—the temporary throne room, as those quarters were now identified!

Stopped by several officious military officers, I played my high card and identified myself. They immediately attempted to arrest me. I foiled them by announcing that I had arrested myself! I had come voluntarily, with my followers, to await the pleasure of the new king of Atlantis.

What could they possibly say?

Pytho's chambers were drafty and squalid. I observed much dirty linen, numerous empty wineskins, and small pots of cosmetics suspiciously like those worn by the late captain.

Aphrodisia expressed concern about my status, now that I had arrested myself. I assured her it was but a clever, meaningless legalism. Conax wondered how meaningless, calling my attention to the fact that squads of soldiers jammed the outer corridor.

On my advice, the barbarian had surrendered his sword to the officers. Now he began to complain that his good mood had made him act rashly.

Of all our party, Mrf Qqt was by far the most composed. He seated himself on a cushion, his cowl thrown back, the silver disc gleaming on his forehead. If all my acquaintances trusted me as completely, I thought, how pleasant and unruffled my existence would be!

Some while later—it was impossible to tell how advanced the day had become, due to the rainy darkness—an impressive tootle of pipes announced Pytho.

He marched into the room still wearing his armor. It glistened with rain, as did his hair, on which reposed the new imperial circlet. He wore ribands of black around his right and left arms, right and left kneecaps, throat and forehead—that was overdoing public grief a bit, I thought!

I had previously instructed Mrf Qqt on the necessity for abasement. He performed it awkwardly, just behind me. Pytho seated himself in a cross-legged chair. His scarred face appeared relaxed, even genial. Once I caught a whiff of his breath, I knew why.

"Well, well, Hoptor the Vintner. Self-arrested! This has been a day of wonders. We gather this peculiar blue person is one of the marvelous beings about whom you communicated with our late monarch?"

"That's correct," I replied. "We regret exceedingly the passing of His Exaltedness—"

"We are certain you do," Pytho said. His eyes gave me a shiver, I don't mind admitting!

He picked at his teeth, then belched. Wine fumes clouded round my head. He was so deep in his cups, he wasn't even startled by the appearance of Mrf Qqt.

He resumed, "We were totally unprepared for the honor which the late Geriasticus placed on our shoulders. In fact, we urged him to grant rule to his consort. But concerned for the health of her person, especially under the constant pressures of statecraft, he deemed her too precious to bear the burden—"

How smoothly the rascal dissembled! Aphrodisia snorted at the last remark, but Pytho was too intoxicated to notice.

"Thus the palm passed to us, just as our monarch succumbed to the last wracking phases of flux. Alas, there was not even time to summon a physician." He wiped a crocodile tear from his eye.

Then he clapped his hands for wine. The serving boy, cold sober, swooned at the sight of His Subservience. Three more had to be summoned, before one was found with stamina to perform the requested task.

I found Pytho's wine-soaked state not a bit unusual. He was merry, and well he might be! None would ever know what had really transpired in the king's last hour. Flux? Never. More like the dirk, the cup—or a pillow jammed over the old ruler's breathing orifices. Of that I grew more and more certain.

However, I had other matters in hand.

"Your Exaltedness, your humble servant hopes you'll permit bygones to be bygones—"

"It's possible," he returned, with a cryptic stare.

"Might I ask—did you perchance confer with Geriasticus over the matter of the Zorophim?"

"Those blue things, you mean? Yes, he reported some of it to us. But refresh our memory, Hoptor."

At once I did so. I painted a glowing portrait of the Zorophim, outlined the advantages of a peaceful meeting between heads of state, touched upon the matter of the Sacred Fuel, and concluded with some telling suggestions about ways and means to use the meeting to quiet the disorderly populace. At the close, I pressed into his hands the small tablet, writ by Geriasticus. All in all, a flawless performance!

"You say these Zorophim wish to acquaint themselves with the scientific lore of our Island Kingdom?" Pytho asked between swills of wine.

"That is our entire purpose," confirmed His Subservience.

"We come in peace, seeking wellsprings of the Sacred Fuel, as our Official Liaison Officer mentioned."

"Then we'll be delighted to cooperate! As Hoptor has suggested, your arrival will have a salutary effect upon the masses. Bid your rulers land. Have them bring their miraculous craft down right in the main courtyard. We deem it wisest for only one craft to land at first, in order that the public can get accustomed to the idea. Invite the rest to descend tomorrow. Naturally we guarantee the safety of all aboard."

Mrf Qqt bowed in stately fashion. "That is good news indeed. It shall be communicated to the almighty ones at once."

So saying, he touched blue fingers to the silver disc. I leaped forward to forestall the communication.

"One moment, one moment please! There remain a few trifling minor matters—the reward on my unfortunate head, for one. I'm the Official Liaison Officer now. So I beseech the king to usher in a new era of justice by pardoning one and all in my party. In return for this magnanimous gesture"— (I nearly choked on the noxious syllables. Expediency is expediency, however!) —"we pledge loyalty to the house of Pytho I."

His brutish fingers touched the imperial circlet.

"Yesterday, we would have refused. Today—well, it's as they say. The office of king changes a man. Grants him new perspectives and attitudes in a twinkling. You are all pardoned in full. Now please make haste to invite the almighty ones to descend. We are most anxious to learn how they propel their sky-craft. Yes indeed, we certainly are!"

Overjoyed that I had pulled it off, I never paused to wonder at the rapidity of Pytho's conversion. Puffed up with my success, I permitted Mrf Qqt to touch the silver disc.

Evidently he communicated with his rulers by a sort of silent wiggling of his jaws. He soon informed us that the Zorophimian monarchs would descend to the courtyard that very day.

Before nightfall, an imperial tympani corps boomed the welcome. Whole regiments of troops had been turned out. The luminescent vessel came glittering downward in the rain. Government employees were stationed everywhere, including the rooftops. They had been given the rest of the day off, and instructed to wave bandananas, throw flowers, and cheer lustily. My friends and I occupied a post of honor near the ceremonial carpet upon which Pytho I would receive his guests.

113

The craft settled on its tripod legs. The hatchway opened. The incline dropped down.

Then the familiar figures of His Splendor and Her Radiance appeared, to the gasps and applause of the multitude.

The royal pair descended the incline, then advanced to the carpet over which a canopy was being held.

Resplendent in his robes of state, Pytho I marched forward with a dozen armed guards. A wide grin split his battered face.

"O miraculous moment!" Babylos whispered at my elbow. "The old order changeth—"

So I thought too, in that last fleeting moment of innocence.

His Exaltedness Pytho I bowed to the smiling blue monarchs. Smile locked in place, he came upright. He remarked through clenched teeth:

"All right, boys, grab them!"

Whereupon, with weapons bared, his bodyguard leaped forward to surround the Zorophim!

✳ Thirteen ✳

While I gasped in horror, the armored plug-uglies menaced Zorop's rule with broadswords and spears. Smug satisfaction caused Pytho's scars to purple, a colorful effect I knew all too well.

At my side, His Subservience Mrf Qqt whispered:

"Is this some ploy of yours, Vintner? Some trick designed to gain you an advantage—?"

"Believe me, I hadn't the slightest inkling—! You heard me receive the king's personal guarantees—!"

Conax growled, "As an adviser on statecraft, baboon-belly, you're as effective as a cake of ice in hell."

"Very well, turn on me! I only did my best, that's all! I only tried, that's all! Curse me, scourge me—how was I to know that we couldn't trust him?"

But of course, on reflection, I knew I should have been more wary. If I maneuvered events in my favor, why not Pytho, who had a record far more reprehensible than mine?

Conax's thews began to quiver fitfully, indicating that he

might unleash his temper at any moment. Then he seemed to think better of it. Good thing, too; even the fighting fury of a full roused barbarian couldn't have coped with the companies of armed men in the courtyard.

His Exaltedness, Pytho I, had grown aware of our buzzing. He turned to glare at us, just as Mrf Qqt reached for the disc on his forehead.

"I shall summon the fleet," he confided. "Perhaps we Zorophim may not survive the day. But before we wing to the Eternal Bonko"—at least I believe that was his term!—"we'll be avenged. We are slow to provoke, but once we are—"

"Hold, hold, Your Subservience! Don't you see we're completely surrounded? Call down your ships now and you invite instant death for your monarchs!"

He hesitated, his blue fingers quite near the disc. Out beneath the canopy, His Splendor and Her Radiance flexed their digits frantically—as if this friendly gesture could make all the surrounding swords disappear!

In the hatchway of their craft, other Zorophim could be seen, conversing with obvious alarm. They too recognized the threat of the sword-ring, and did no more than whisper among themselves.

"Surely," I heard His Splendor address Pytho, "surely there has been some error of protocol—?"

"We doubt that," Pytho sneered.

"But you personally guaranteed a friendly welcome!"

"So we lied." Pytho shrugged. "It served our purposes. Don't tell me you've never done the same in your empire! Too bad you'll never return to wherever that is!"

Then he fixed me with a baleful eye.

"As for your so-called Liaison Officer, you were ill-advised to listen to him. He has long been at the top of our list of undesirables. About the only liaison he can arrange is between a nobleman and one of his wenches. He's an inept schemer—far more stupid than we originally believed! Trust our promises? How foolish! As to your disposition, excellencies, you shall be conducted to apartments in the palace. There, our number one torturer will interrogate you."

Then, with a broad gesture: "Bring chains! And secure their vessel until we discover its motive power!"

Soldiers rushed forward bearing manacles and leg irons. His Splendor and Her Radiance were unceremoniously shackled, even as another platoon invaded their shining craft. Shortly, every last blue being was turned out into the open. Each was restrained by one or more chains.

In a sad procession led by His Splendor and Her Radiance, the Zorophim were escorted from the yard.

Pytho I remained behind, leering with glee. I discovered the reason for his delay when the Zorophim had all but clanked out of sight.

Pytho glanced at the sky. It had begun to darken again. He signed me forward.

"Who, me?" Inexplicably, my feet bore me backward. "The king can't wish to speak to lowly m—yow!"

A sword in my backside shot me forward. I had trouble abasing myself properly, due to a sudden onslaught of palsy.

"Stand up, you swollen son of the sewers!" His Exaltedness cried, seizing my hair. I was on my feet instantly, I'll tell you!

I observed Pytho darting glances at the crowds still assembled. Then he said:

"We feel we owe you a certain debt, Vintner. You have delivered a prize into our hands."

"Unwillingly and unwittingly!" I said. Of course I regretted my remark at once. He cuffed me, and shrieked for silence.

Then, regaining his control, he said, "No doubt you're wondering about the purpose of the seizure you just witnessed."

"I suppose you plan to make the Zorophim the feature attraction at some terrible court orgy of cruel depravity—"

"Don't you give us credit for greater wit than that? We intend to relieve them of their various secrets. What propels yon magical craft, for instance? By what arcane principles is it levitated above the rooftops? Once we possess this marvelous information, we shall dispose of the blue creatures. But not before. For fat and foolish as you are, Vintner, your brain still contains a kernel of perception. Currently we hold the throne by force. The populace is restless, affrighted. Firmly in control of the scientific secrets of Zorop—and sharing those secrets with none!—we can easily convince the rabble that we possess divine power. They'll think twice about open rebellion. Fear is a powerful deterrent. Superstitious fear twice so. Perhaps, to exploit that fact to full advantage, we'll even have ourselves elevated to godhood. So you see—you have been helpful to our cause after all! As a token of our appreciation, we intend to grant you a boon."

"You intend to spare my friends and me? Oh, thank you, Your Exaltedness—"

"Spare you? Naturally not! Our boon is this. Rather than a lingering death, lasting for days and including excruciating agonies, you shall, by our grace, be dispatched promptly, with

116

as little mess and bother as possible. A splendid gift, is it not, Hoptor?"

As he tittered in cruel mockery, I realized I'd been gulled once again!

Pytho treated me to a merry wave. "Good-bye, now, and good luck to you. Give our regards to Hades—or wherever it is you go! By the way—you haven't seen Captain Num, have you? That little tease has quite disappeared."

Unable to speak, I shook my head.

With a shrug, Pytho remarked, "No matter. He's rather beneath us, now that we have our new status." And he stumped off toward the palace, surrounded by three dozen armored thugs.

I stood miserably beneath the canopy, which was beginning to sway in the stiff wind. I glanced at the shining vessel, now guarded by several soldiers. Throughout the courtyard, the crowds were dispersing. But my unhappy companions still waited, along with yet another military detachment.

"You've good news?" Aphrodisia asked as I approached. "The king's spared us, isn't that right, Hoptor?"

"Uh, well, not exactly—"

I was spared the necessity of further explanation by a sudden surge of the soldiers around us. Their callous expressions and coarse jests made our fate instantly apparent.

With a bellow, Conax began to struggle, managing to snap a few wrists and blacken a few eyes before he was borne to the ground. Thus unmanned, he was shackled round the ankles and dragged over the stones in the wake of our group.

Aphrodisia lost no chance to heap abuse on my head.

"Oh, Hoptor, you've failed again! How I regret that I ever allowed you to lure me into the vintage trade! Of course I lost my heart to you because of your glib tongue and seemingly superior education. Who was I, a mere schoolgirl with an attractive body, to see that honeyed phrases often prove powerless? If we're to be sentenced to death once more, the very least you can do is let me die as a fulfilled female. Five minutes with a priest and we can face the funeral pyre as husband and wife—"

"Yes, yes, naturally," I said, my mind being elsewhere; namely, upon the problem of how we could save ourselves this time. Of course I was once again held responsible for our plight—as if I could outsmart every last blackguard in Atlantis! The others looked to me for leadership, and I was wracking my brain for a scheme. Thus I agreed with Aphrodisia, while hardly hearing her.

117

"Hoptor! Do you truly mean it this time?"

"What? Oh, of course. As soon as we devise a means of escape—"

"Not another delay, surely—!"

"Come, Aphrodisia, which do you prefer? Being a living fugitive or a wedded corpse?"

"Considering the trials you've put me through lately, the latter has much to recommend it. You realize you have now promised—"

"And I'll honor that vow the instant we're free, if you'll just be silent and permit me to think!"

In truth, I was beginning to see the glimmers of a plan. Not much of one, I must admit privately! But the best I could concoct on the spur of the moment.

I mulled it furiously as we were led back to the prison building, descending to the very dungeon cell we had occupied before. One of the guards—a large-headed lout with a walleye —gave Aphrodisia a lascivious look as old Menos greeted us.

Naturally Menos expressed his regrets. Then he carefully pointed out that he could again be of no help. This time also, the death order had been issued by the supreme ruler.

"But do you know how much time we've got?" I inquired as he clanked the door shut.

Locking it, he tossed the key to Walleye. "No scroll has arrived as yet. But I'm anticipating the issuance of the document momentarily. I expect it will call for execution before sunrise."

"What, execute one of your oldest, dearest friends? The one who spared you humiliation in the matter of the birthmark—?"

"Don't start that again, Hoptor! I tell you there's nothing I can do! Naturally I couldn't bring myself to lop off your head personally. I shall let that sad duty fall to Cloddus."

He indicated Walleye, who continued to lounge nearby, letting his hot, if skewed, eyeballs rove up and down Aphrodisia's frame. She noticed the unwelcome attention.

"How dare you strip me with your eyes, you cur? I'm practically a married woman!"

I let that one pass.

In the grimy reaches of the cell, Conax was busily gnashing his teeth, having recovered from being dragged across the stones. Babylos seemed to have sunk into a daze. He squatted in a corner, prattling more of his warnings of destruction. I certainly wished I had his detachment! I no longer gave one

118

olive seed for the welfare of fair Atlantis. Not with my own to concern me!

Menos seemed reluctant to leave us.

"You must understand, Hoptor old fellow, I wouldn't even want to know about your execution, had I others to stand in for me. But I've been stripped of all my prison manpower. Except for Cloddus yonder, of course. Poor fellow, he was left behind because he always casts a spear at the oblique. That sad condition of his eyes, you understand—"

Cloddus' eyes didn't seem in all that bad shape! Both were still busily engaged examining Aphrodisia's physical charms. But the remark of Menos piqued my interest in another way. I drew him aside in order to whisper:

"What is the reason for this reduction of prison manpower?"

"Riots, of course. They're breaking out almost hourly. In every quarter! I believe old Babylos, as well as the lesser prophets of doom, have done their work thoroughly. Torrential rains are falling again, and the populace is convinced that Atlantis is accursed. It takes a huge number of troops to quell all the outbreaks—"

I digested this information quickly, as it might well aid my skimpy plan. But I would need to move fast. Pytho would waste no time extracting the secrets of the Zorophim. Having discovered how to levitate their craft, for instance, he would probably whiz it up for a flight—and spread the word that he was at the controls!

Once the public believed he was privy to such powers, they'd heel soon enough. We had to act before it happened.

"Well, Menos"— a contrived yawn—"that's interesting, certainly. But it hardly affects me any longer. I believe I shall lie down and take a nap."

"Sleep only hours before your life is snuffed out? How can you, Hoptor?"

"To a man at peace with himself," I lied, "death is not the least fearful. Good evening."

That I was able to utter such a ridiculous statement proves my desperation just then! Had Menos happened to glance down at my knees, he would have known my deception.

Instead, he merely sighed sadly. As he departed, he told me:

"Right after I have my supper, I'll see whether the execution order's come down."

But I was already at work hustling Aphrodisia into a corner, signaling both Conax and Mrf Qqt to follow. Old Babylos I left to himself, rambling of the coming apocalypse.

"Pay attenion, all of you. We must act while Menos is off having his meal. There's no one left guarding us save for Cloddus." Quickly I expained my proposal.

"That's only another of your schemes that will come to naught," scoffed Conax.

"Can you suggest a better one? If so, you have the floor!"

"I—" Scarlet climbed in his cheeks. Naturally he fell silent. Aphrodisia, too, looked critical.

"If I understand your outline, Hoptor, the entire first stage depends on me."

"That's quite right, sweetheart," I said, stroking her hand in my most ingratiating way. "None of the rest of us is—ah —equipped for the task."

"Well, I won't do it! You have led me into debauchery too often. I intend to reform before meeting the gods. I shall confront them as a married woman of spotless character."

"May I remind you that if my plan works, it won't be necessary to confront the gods?"

"I'd rather do that than what you're suggesting!"

"Well, Aphrodisia"—my final ploy!—"if that's your attitude, I'll just have to renege on my promise—"

"Your promise?"

"Of marriage. A promise which, until this moment, I fully intended to honor. But it's obvious you don't love me anymore. Don't respect my brain. Care nothing for my welfare—!"

"But I do, Hoptor—against my better judgment! Can't you understand that's why I want to abandon the vintage trade forever? I want to be a wife you can be proud of!"

"In order for that to happen, Aphrodisia, I must be alive and breathing. Please, dear—one last time, for all our sakes. Think of His Subservience—Conax the king—that gentle old philosopher crooning there in the corner—will you condemn them all, when to save them you need only ply your talents for a moment?"

Frankly, I am convinced that my eloquence was as responsible for her decision—more!—as my pledge to wed her; sobbing, she at last relented.

I coached her in a matter of moments.

The rest of us retired to assigned positions, leaving Aphrodisia to do her work. She pressed her contours against the bars, and uttered an attention-getting moan.

I leaned against a nearby wall, eyes closed as though I dozed on my feet. But I could observe the torchlit corridor.

After her second moan, Cloddus appeared. He stopped well

120

clear of the bars, licking his lips and ogling Aphrodisia shamelessly.

"Something troubling you, darling?" he asked, hardly able
to conceal his lust.

"Yes. Oh, yes, officer!"

"I'm not an officer, dear. But you can call me one if you
want to."

"You look like you should be an officer."

"Do you really think so?"

"Oh, yes, very definitely."

I congratulated myself upon my training skills; she was
acting the courtesan most convincingly—no small assignment,
given the setting!

Cloddus swelled up like a toad at the flattery. Aphrodisia
continued:

"I know you can do nothing to stop the execution, since
the order's coming from His Exaltedness personally. But dying
would be far easier to bear if I had a sip or two of wine first.
In fact, I would be willing to do virtually anything for just
one refreshing draft."

Cloddus turned red with excitement. "That is—do you
mean—you would step down the hall to my booth? Drink
the wine there, before prudish Menos returns?"

"Anything, anything!" Aphrodisia panted, overacting a bit
now, in my opinion.

But Cloddus was blind to all subtleties. He sidled up to the
bars and reached through, gargling some lewd endearment.
At that precise moment, I sounded the call to action!

Aphrodisia seized Cloddus by the ears. Conax sprang forward and bent the fellow's arm around a bar. His Subservience
thwacked the side of Cloddus' head. This rendered him unconscious instantly.

On my knees, I snagged the key from his belt, just before
he collapsed like a felled tree.

"Oh!" Aphrodisia exclaimed. "I've never felt so degraded
in my life! I know I have done far worse in my time. But
I've already assumed the mental attitude for marriage. Hoptor,
when—?"

"Hurry, Conax, now it's your turn!" I broke in, pointing
to the unlocked door. "Hie yourself to those places you've
memorized—you have memorized them, haven't you?"

"Yes, but I'm not accustomed to such heavy mental work.
I look forward to the hour when I can call upon my thews—"

"But you can't use your thews till we rouse the populace
into complete revolt! To do that, it's essential that you spread

121

the story I gave you—Pytho plans a regime of terror and increased taxes. You must also say that, at this very hour, he's drawing up a document to place all of Atlantis under martial law. Those rumors, planted in the proper quarters, should increase the rioting fivefold. However, you must be certain that you reach the opinion leaders I have listed. Repeat the name and location of each."

"Scribblus, editor-in-chief of the *Weekly Tablet*. He's found at—uh—number two, Quill Lane. The Holex, supreme priest of the Atlantean High Church."

"Where?"

"At the sign of the Golden Stew."

"Pew!"

"Sorry."

"Be sure to advise Holex that Pytho also intends to overthrow the state religion, installing demon worship instead. The third of the opinion leaders is—?"

"The head of the Robbers' Guild, at number—number—gods, I've no head for this!"

"Number twelve, Rotten Row. You can do it, Conax. You must! Your speed and strength will carry you to all points in an hour. And we'll have the population up in arms for fair—provided that, in each case, you don't forget to mention my name. Only that will validate the statements!"

I hauled the cell door open.

"We'll leave Babylos to his visions. Aphrodisia, you come with me. You also, Your Subservience. I need that lethal fist for the next stage of my plan."

A shadow appeared on the stair wall. But with one tap, Mrf Qqt sent Menos to slumber. Ignoring the other prisoners demanding release, we crept upward in stealthy fashion, through a prison empty of guards.

We emerged into the great courtyard, where another downpour had indeed erupted. I sprang into action despite the bad omen, for the success of the next phase was entirely my responsibility.

✳ Fourteen ✳

From beyond the palace wall, we clearly heard the cries of mobs, and this despite the noise of the rain. I was encouraged that the seeds I had bade Conax plant would fall on fertile soil.

I gave a keen glance to all points of the courtyard. A dismal, drenched place, save for the far quarter. There, the craft of the Zorophim glowed, illuminating the darkness roundabout it. The light also revealed four sodden soldiers pacing up and down.

My plan depended upon learning the whereabouts of the Zorophimian rulers. I suspected only a person of some authority would know. This dictated a wait, until a captain of guards chanced to appear.

He kept his head down, cursing the rain roundly. As he passed our gloomy doorway, I leaped forward.

With speed born of desperation, I snaked one hand around his waist. I hauled out his sword while my other arm crooked his neck.

He was a powerful, hot-tempered rascal, and would have tossed me off like a gnat, had I not managed to impress the point of his blade into his back.

"Stand still, unless you wish to meet your ancestors tonight!"

He cursed again, but did not struggle.

"Now tell me—where is Pytho torturing the blue king and queen?"

"His Exaltedness returned them to yon vessel for the night."

"What? So soon? If you're lying, lout—"

"With that iron stabbing my guts?"

"Very well, thanks for your cooperation. Your Subservience? Your fist, if you please."

One tap and the captain slept.

I donned his armorplate—a tight fit, I must confess!—and, dragging the man's soggy cloak over my head, I whispered instructions to Mrf Qqt.

Of quick mind, he understood at once. Tugging Aphrodisia's hand, he started out to circle the courtyard. I wished fervently that another person could be found to perform all these acts of derring-do; my belly was shaky as a pudding.

Had it been merely a matter of garnering medals, or risking life and limb for some collection of patriotic slogans, I would have been away like a shot! But self-interest works many wonders.

Thus I strutted forward into the eerie light cast by the vessel. Its side hatchway, I was pleased to see, had not yet been closed for the night.

The nearest soldier challenged me at once. Feigning arrogance, I waved him aside.

"That's all right, corporal, hold your post. Captain Bolvolio here. Secret service. Come to inspect the security of the quarters of those blue horrors. Direct order from His Exaltedness—"

Talking nonstop, I proceeded past him, straight to the incline.

"—Our new king wants to make sure that his royal guests can't escape. I'll handle the check, so at ease, at ease!"

Waving grandly, I started to walk up the incline—far harder than walking down. After two steps, I tumbled down on my backside.

A couple of the guards sniggered. I glared.

"Eyes front! Else your relatives will hear the secret service knocking on their doors at midnight!"

So saying, I seized the edges of the incline and scuttled up, crab-fashion.

As I gained the halfway point, one guard remarked to another:

"Have you ever heard of an organization known as the secret service?"

"No, I haven't heard of a Captain Bolvolio, either. And I've mustered in and around the palace for twenty-two years! Hmm, I wonder—"

Three-quarters of the way up! And scrabbling and sliding on the rain-slicked incline for all I was worth!

"Say, look at his sandals, will you? By the gods, those aren't military issue—!"

"Halt, Captain Bolvolio—if that's your name! I said *halt*—!"

I tumbled forward into the marvelous craft, while halloos and hammering boots sounded behind. All four guards were coming after me!

In a perfect delirium of terror, I banged at this locked door, then the next. I rushed around a bend in the corridor, and immediately encountered two blue beings. His Splendor and Her Radiance!

I believe they also recognized me. But I was not about to exchange pleasantries, as the four soldiers were pounding in pursuit. A portal presented itself on the left. I hurled myself through with all the force at my disposal.

O unhappy maneuver! At once, my feet flew out from under me—and I slid down an incline I remembered well.

Grasping at nonexistent hand holds, I struck bottom, rolled across the narrow gallery to its edge, and dropped over!

As I plummeted, I tried to make peace with the gods, begging forgiveness for my many moral errors.

Then I struck, splashed, and sank.

As the dark liquid closed over me, I realized I had fallen into a vat of the Sacred Fuel. Despite my thrashings, I continued to sink. All at once, though, my sandals touched bottom. I kicked out mightily and—lo!—I surfaced.

Purple liquid rivered off my brows, ran down my cheeks, and dripped from the tip of my nose. A pungent aroma assailed me then. I stuck out my tongue to catch a drop of Sacred Fuel. I tasted it. Then I tasted another.

Finally, I scooped some up in my palm. Already reeling from its fragrance, I swallowed a good mouthful. My brain burst with the shock of recognition!

"There's the impostor—seize him!" howled a soldier who had just poked his head through the doorway above. "Stop shoving me, you damned dogs! There's no stair here, only—"

But the thrust of those behind him proved irresistible. With a shriek of terror, he whizzed down the incline, rolled across the gallery, and created a tidal wave in my vat.

The other three soldiers remained crowded at the door. I didn't understand their lack of coordination until I spied a blue head adorned by tufts of hair. I cried huzzah for the plucky queen of the Zorophim as, employing her lethal fist, she launched the soldiers down the incline.

Dripping and fragrant, I clambered out of the vat just as the second man fell in. His companions followed at brief intervals.

While the quartet thrashed and swore, I scuttled for a hand-ladder which took me up to the gallery. There, I dashed to the incline. From the top, His Splendor and Her Radiance looked down.

Her Radiance asked her husband, "Why is the Vintner giggling at such a desperate moment?"

125

"Perhaps the melee has damaged his mind."

"Not at all, to the contrary! I am thinking with wonderful clarity. And I've just discovered a marvelous secret. But give me a hand. We must escape at once!"

In the vat, the soldiers were punching each other fiercely. The sharpest of them discovered that I was not among the punchees. Dashing purple liquid from his eyes, he sighted me and yelled.

His fellows paid little attention. They had started scooping up double handfuls of Sacred Fuel, and were consuming it with gusto. The leader once more cried for pursuit. The drinkers howled merry obscenities.

Accepting assistance from His Splendor, I regained the top of the incline. Down below, the soldiers continued to swill and frolic.

"This is a calamity of the highest order!" cried Her Radiance as we shut the door and made it fast. "The Sacred Fuel has been profaned!"

"No religious fanaticism, please! We have larger matters to worry about! Follow me and we'll check the situation outside."

Happily, no additional soldiers had arrived, As we descended the incline, I promised the blue monarchs that I knew a safe place.

Two rain-drenched figures appeared from the darkness— Mrf Qqt and Aphrodisia. The latter flung her arms around my neck.

"Oh, Hoptor, we thought you slain—!"

"Please, please, let's get out of this light. At any moment, some soldier may glance our way—"

So saying, I hustled them all into the shadows.

We crouched by the outer wall as a company pelted by, armed to the jowls with swords, dirks, tridents, and spears. At quick time, the soldiers dashed out the nearest gate. Ordered forth to put down a new civil disorder, perhaps?

Just then, I realized the rain had stopped. I glanced up past the lamplit palace to a murky sky. A light wind blew, riffling rain puddles. Was this the calm before the storm's full fury? I don't mind admitting I shivered!

"Halp! Ho!—assistance, someone—!"

A purple-dyed soldier appeared in the hatchway of the craft. He weaved on his feet, and suddenly tittered. Off balance, he fell and slid down the incline. I was positive that, among his companions remaining inside, there would be none

126

who had not been overcome by Sacred Fuel. We were momentarily safe.

Thus I urged my charges toward the nearby gate.

Another soldier popped out of a booth and attempted to interrogate us. I captured his interest with my pose as Captain Bolvolio. Drenched purple and in utter disarray, I couldn't carry off the deception for more than an instant. But that was ample time for Mrf Qqt to use his fist.

"Haste, haste!" I exclaimed, shoving the others past the slumbering guard.

"Where are we going?" asked Mrf Qqt.

"To my villa."

"We wonder if that will be a safe haven," His Splendor said.

"As safe as any this topsy-turvy night. Besides, there's something I must show you. After that's taken care of, we can provision ourselves, slip away into the city and await developments."

But as we rushed unmolested through the first shadowy boulevard, developments soon became perfectly clear.

Down a side street we saw another riot; several hundred persons were involved. Two buildings had been fired, and the sky-leaping flames showed some soldiers getting the worst of it.

Again and again on our dash to my house, we witnessed similar disorders in progress. Many fires were being set. The underbellies of the clouds glared scarlet. I began to entertain hope that with disorder rampant, Pytho I might be forced to overlook our escape.

I asked a question which had been puzzling me:

"How did your excellencies fare with Pytho's number one torturer? There isn't a mark visible on either of you."

"Naturally not," returned Her Radiance. "The infernal devices of the master torturer never touched our persons."

"How can that be, unless you revealed secrets?"

"We revealed what that scar-faced lord of misrule believed to be secrets," His Splendor said. "A meaningless podge of noddle and smarf"—— I believe those were the terms he used! ——"a nursery babble, in a bastard mixture of our tongue and yours. But it set that villain Pytho crying for a corps of translators. They scribbled our every utterance on their tablets. Then they rushed away to decipher the transcript. We wish them good fortune! But we venture that several will lose their heads. All they'll come up with is gibberish."

"Pytho couldn't tell the difference, eh?"

"Power-mad monarchs are easily deceived, Hoptor. They believe chiefly what they wish to believe. And Pytho wished to believe that, being cowards, we would of course surrender our higher knowledge. Happily, we have none like him on Zorop. Of course, not all Atlanteans are as bad as he," the king added, somewhat hastily. "You have obviously tried to do your best by us—"

"And shall continue to do so, you may be assured! Quick, now, take a right. My villa is but a few squares straight on."

Thus, while the wind keened, bringing sounds of alarm and odors of burning from nearly every quarter, we arrived at our destination. I discovered that my villa's front doors had been wrenched completely off. By looters or the military, I couldn't say which.

Inside, I dared light but one lamp. That was sufficient for my purposes, however.

From my study I fetched mortar and pestle. I asked Aphrodisia to hold the lamp high, and led the way into the garden.

There, in a transport of expectation, I rushed among the damaged vines, managing to locate a few surviving grapes. I quickly scraped off most of the mold and thrust the grapes into the pestle. Then I crushed them with my mortar.

Trembling, I extended the utensils to His Splendor. I bade him taste of the pulp clinging to the pestle.

This he did, and fell to his knees, a beatific expression on his face.

"O astonishment and wonder! It is the Sacred Fuel!"

"Why, yes," I replied, "unless my nose and tongue mislead me."

Aphrodisia, for one, couldn't believe it.

"Do you mean to suggest that those marvelous vessels are propelled by the fruit of the lowly grape?"

"I mean to suggest exactly that. I fell in a vat of the stuff a while ago, and received the shock of recognition. Why do you think those soldiers were lurching and tittering when they should have been busy chasing us? They were intoxicated by Sacred Fuel! Don't ask me to explain further, because I'm not conversant with matters scientific. But isn't it obvious—?"

I lowered my voice, and pointed; both His Splendor and Her Radiance were kneeling, once more tasting of the pulpy pestle.

"—I've given these important personages the treasure they sought. That is why I wished to return to the villa. In these disorganized times, we need every friend we can get!"

"Blessed be the name of Hoptor of Atlantis!" Her Radiance wore a positively worshipful expression.

"Blessed, blessed!" affirmed her consort.

To which I replied smoothly, "I trust you won't forget to mention my name when it comes time to dispense any appropriate rewards—"

At which Aphrodisia shrieked.

"I know you're excited by this fabulous discovery, dear. However, please try to—oh good gods!"

Helmeted heads looked over the garden wall. And before I could say "Island Kingdom," a half dozen more scaling ladders appeared.

"He's here, Your Exaltedness," rose the cry from without.

"Into the house!" I exclaimed. But it was too late. More soldiers were coming from there. In a trice we were encircled.

Wheezing and huffing, clad in full battle armor, Pytho popped into sight on one of the ladders. Already his men were jumping down into the garden, trampling my precious vines and menacing us with swords. Mrf Qqt struck a few telling blows with his fist. But the soldiers quickly learned to avoid it, and several seized him from behind. In like fashion, the king and queen were rendered helpless.

Another ladder was handed over the wall, then positioned so that Pytho might descend with some dignity. He stumped up to me, jutting his scar-marked jaw.

"You have eluded us for the last time, you traitor. We shall now give you what you so richly deserve."

Aphrodisia wailed, "I thought you said he'd be too busy to chase us, Hoptor!"

"Gods, it was only a guess—!"

"A wrong one," jeered Pytho. "These bestial blue horrors"—the Zorophim didn't take kindly to that!—"represent our strongest hold upon an already antic populace. We need their supernatural wisdom in order to terrorize our subjects into submission—"

"How are your savants coming along with the translation of the secrets we have already given you?" inquired His Splendor.

"They had better be coming along just swimmingly, else they'll lose their heads!" Pytho signed to some of his men. "These blue nightmares are to be returned to the palace. Unmolested. However, the two treacherous Atlanteans—hold." He leered at Aphrodisia. "No. Only one shall die. Since that fickle Captain Num has apparently deserted us, perhaps, to befit our new, kingly image, we should renew interest in the opposite sex. As you ascend to the gods, Vintner—or, more likely, descend to the infernal regions!—you can amuse

129

yourself with the vision of this charming child locked in our embrace—"

And he began to pinch and fondle her in the most shameless fashion!

"No, no, kill me too!" she protested. "I want to die right along with Hoptor!"

The little baggage! I could have throttled her for encouraging Pytho's mania for execution.

"Let's waste no more time on this disreputable fellow," he said. "Yonder bench will serve as a handy block. Which one of you wants to act as headsman?"

I was a little discomfited by the way the soldiers vied for the duty, offering oaths and sword flourishes as signs of enthusiasm.

In short order, I was forced to kneel. My head was turned sidewise and my cheek thrust down on chill stone. Above me, he who had won Pytho's nod assumed a wide-legged stance.

"That a man of honest, patriotic character should come to such an untimely end—" I began.

I don't know exactly what I said after that. I was only conscious of my would-be executioner. With both hands upon his hilt, he raised his blade over his head.

"Farewell, Aphrodisia," I may have remarked. "Farewell, noble Zorophim. Farewell, Atlantis, my natal state. May sunny skies one day smile upon you again—"

"He's stalling," Pytho barked. "Get busy and chop his head off."

The sword shimmered high above me. I closed my eyes with a sense of finality.

Thereupon, we heard the call of brazen war horns.

They sounded, it seemed, from all quarters at once. Someone raced by in the street, yelling.

Pytho sent a soldier up a ladder to inquire about the disturbance.

All of us thrilled with amazement as we heard the answer:

"Strange great-sailed war ships, packed to the gunwales with howling men, have landed on the northern shore. The city's defenses are breached!"

From rooftops all around, as the brazen horns kept braying, I heard fresh wails and screams. I also detected many voices uttering ululating war-cries.

"The winegourd of Conax the Chimerical has floated home!" I announced. "His minions have arrived to rescue him, and also to sack, loot, rape, burn, and murder. Whatever happens to me, Pytho—you're finished!"

✳ Fifteen ✳

O what sweet satisfaction pierced me then—instead of the executioner's sword, it's my pleasure to report!

Pytho first uttered a snigger of disbelief. But a moment later, he lapsed into concerned silence as the ululating warcries resounded ever more loudly.

The troops under his command began to exchange fevered glances. Outside the wall, a woman shrilled:

"Run for your lives! The painted invaders are everywhere! My sisters, my aunt, my cousin, and my mother have already been raped repeatedly. Flee, flee, doom's upon us all—!"

Roundabout my villa, many shutters thwacked open. Voices demanded to know whether the alarm was genuine. Then, in a neat touch of meteorological punctuation, the very heavens roared and rocked with thunder.

Lightning flashed brighter than I had ever seen it. The wind immediately began to howl. Pytho's assorted scars drained of color.

In nearby streets, the tumult rose—as did the horrific howls of the barbarians. To this cacaphony was added the distinct sounds of doors being broken open, and citizens being assaulted and abused.

Though trembling badly, Pytho managed to shout:

"We must return and defend the palace! Headsman, finish your business at once!"

"Not on your life!" I shrieked, fastening both hands on the executioner's wrist.

Fired with desperation, I wrested the sword away from him. I began to hew the air vigorously, and it was by cunning design—not merely blind luck, as Aphrodisia insists!—that I etched the former general a cut on the shinbone.

"O gods defend me!" cried he, falling among the vines.

The headsman blanched. "The king's down! We have no leader!"

"Every man for himself—before the barbarians butcher us all!" I exclaimed. I grabbed Aphrodisia's hand and ran.

131

Two of the demoralized soldiers made a pathetic attempt to stop us. A light clout from the fist of His Subservience opened the way handily.

Such a din as we fled! War horns honking, houses being torn asunder, mad mobs pelting to and fro in directionless panic—in truth, as we rushed outside, it was all we could do to avoid being trampled.

We huddled against the outer wall of the house. In a trice, the soldiers—all swagger and conceit just a short while ago!—poured out of the front doorway. They scampered as madly as the populace, I don't mind saying!

"Look, citizens! Soldiers of the rotten, usurpatious king!"

Responding to this outcry by a passing grandmother, a crowd formed in a twinkling. When I espied the grandmother vigorously gouging one soldier's eyes, I knew that Conax the Chimerical had succeeded in planting the rumors. The populace was in open revolt against the establishment!

"This way!" I said. "We must seek the protection of Conax at once. Else we're liable to be murdered along with the current administration!"

Having left the soldiers in a moaning heap, the mob rushed away in the opposite direction. Our party turned right, past the garden wall. Within, I heard Pytho still bellowing for assistance.

Once more the lightning fumed, making the spark-filled skies even brighter. Many more fires had been set. With a little help from the gods, fair Atlantis would soon be rubble!

We seemed to be making excellent progress—we had gone about ten squares toward the central city—when another group of men rounded a corner ahead. From their fur wappings, paint-daubed faces, greasy hair, long spears, wicker shields, and berserk exclamations, I deduced they were not friendly.

"Into this alley," I panted, "we'll—Aphrodisia! For heavens sake watch your footing!"

The baggage had slipped on a fruit peel. As I struggled to help her rise, the barbarian horde charged full speed.

Spears cast by mighty-thewed arms whicked and whacked all around us. "It will take a miracle to save us now!" I observed.

Bless the gods eternally! They heard my plea, and withheld their fury no longer!

Following a mighty boom of thunder, the clouds opened. The deluge which had been long aborning descended at last upon the Island Kingdom.

Indeed, the first moments of rain were so blinding, the barbarians were forced to halt in their tracks. That gave us the chance we needed. We detoured at once down the preselected alley.

Thunder rolled more and more loudly, until it seemed the very night would crack open. In the long run, however, the outpouring of the heavens prevented a greater holocaust. In the rain, the barbarians had trouble telling friend from foe. The fury of their attack temporarily abated. Also, the rain helped extinguish many fires.

But everywhere, it seemed, we encountered mobs in mad flight. And the moment the rain slacked just a little, corps of barbarians commenced demolishing homes and shops again.

By stopping several fleeing citizens and mentioning my name at the top of my lungs, I learned that Conax had last been seen at the Grain Market. We rushed thither, bursting into the square as lightning lit up the heavens.

What a sight we beheld! Broadsword in hand and spattered with gore, the Chimerical warrior was supervising the destruction of the grain stores. But it was not his own force, but rather a mob of rebellious Atlanteans, carrying the huge sacks into the plaza and knifing them open.

As each sack spilled its contents, other citizens pressed forward with captured Atlantean officers. One by one, Pytho's functionaries were jammed headfirst into small mountains of meal. They thrashed only a brief time. It was an effective, if ghastly, means of execution. It unsettled me not a little, I don't mind confessing!

"Conax!" I called, hurrying to him. "You must put a stop to this slaughter. These men are only witless tools of the throne!"

"Hail, Hoptor!" he greeted me, a gruesome grin on his gory face. "I assumed that by now, Crok had claimed you for his own."

"I eluded that fate by a hairbreadth. Obviously you planted the seeds of rebellion well."

"Aye, they sprang up instantly and blossomed full at the arrival of my host. Isn't this a splendid night's work? It rivals the time I led my hot-blooded heroes against the warraks of the wicked wazir."

"Yes, yes, you're doing wonderfully. But I still say these officers don't deserve such a cruel fate. It's Pytho you want."

"That ugly little slug? I received a report about him just moments ago."

"What sort of report?"

"A party of my lads found him wandering in the streets.

133

He was dazed with pain from a wound in his shinbone. My bold-hearted bravos bore him instantly to the seawall."

"What did they do with him there?"

"Threw him off! Your misbegotten monarch is meeting his makers down in the watery depths. You're free of Pytho's oppression at last, Hoptor."

So saying, he clapped me on the back.

Upon regaining my feet and digesting the news, I could not help exclaiming:

"Then fair Atlantis is free also! And there's no further excuse for fighting! You must check your warriors, Conax. Else they'll reduce the city to a ruin."

"Check them? I'm afraid I can't do that. They've been confined aboard ship for weeks. They've built up an insatiable desire to rape, loot, sack, burn, and murder."

"But they're in civilized territory now! If you can't put a brake on the pillage, at least stop these horrible and senseless executions. Pytho's troops will become as mild as household goats, if you'll only tell them their oppressor is dead. Have you any evidence of that fact?"

"Why, yes, if you really think it's important—"

Obviously peeved, he stalked to a nearby granary. Shortly he emerged carrying a grisly object.

"Actually, only the bottom part of Pytho went into the waves. My minions brought me this souvenir."

I'd seen him flourish a head before. But he flourished this one with even greater relish! There was no doubt it was the tyrant, thoroughly deceased.

"Very good, Conax—"

"Thanks, I thought so."

"But see here! Morally, we Atlanteans are on your side. It's not fair to continue slaughtering and plundering once the prime target is removed."

"Crok curse your oiled tongue! You're always trying to spoil a fellow's fun!"

But under the pressure of my arguments, he finally relented.

First he called a halt to the suffocations. Then he displayed Pytho's head to the officers who had been spared. They flung off their armor to a man. Some even cried impromptu slogans about Atlantean liberty.

"Satisfied?" Conax barked.

"Not quite! You must send messengers into every quarter—enlist those officers for the assignment. They must convey your personal message that your barbarians refrain from doing a but minimum damage. Come, come, stop pouting! You're still the hero of the hour!"

This leavened his gloom a little. And the officers responded eagerly to his call for volunteers. Thus, not long after it had begun, the furious revolt began to grind to a halt.

By the first light of morning, fair Atlantis had quieted. The fires were out. And no one shrieked in the steadily falling rain.

Still, it had been a devastating night.

As I wandered from street to street, this became more and more clear. Virtually all of the Island Kingdom had been reduced to wreckage. The more flimsy structures had been razed entirely. In less fragile buildings, interiors had been burned to cinders, or flooded by the torrential rains. It would literally take years to restore it all. Not to mention a small fortune!

I walked on, through crowds of sobbing citizens who had returned to their homes, only to find them unlivable. Conditions were the same all over fair Atlantis—sad outcome indeed for a so-called victory!

✶ Sixteen ✶

By noonday, the rain ceased altogether. But by then, most of the streets ran hock-deep in water. It became necessary for the water works staff to open four seawall valves during the period of low tide. Thus the excess drained away.

Meantime, experts from the palace architectural office completed a rapid survey. The news spread within an hour—they estimated it would take on the order of seven hundred and fifty thousand zebs to make necessary repairs to all damaged property. A hasty accounting revealed something less than twenty-two hundred zebs in the treasury—though this was hardly surprising, given the profligate ways of the late Gernasticus. Plainly, Atlantis had been destroyed virtually overnight. This inspired several fresh riots.

As to the leadership of the government, it fell upon the shoulders of wool-witted Babylos!

He had turned up wandering in a bemused state at dawn.

Though I attempted to secure the position for myself, I had no luck. Probably because the fickle public seized on the fact that almost all of Babylos' prophecies had come to pass. Therefore he was venerated instantly by a confused and alarmed populace, and invited to closet himself in the gutted palace with the leaders of the Zorophim.

In this manner, an uneasy day drew to a close.

We Atlanteans were free. But we were also destitute. And we had not the means to rebuild our kingdom, unless we all migrated to distant lands, secured jobs, and regularly sent home a portion of our wages. I, for one, found the very suggestion appalling!

At dusk I went to the palace along with thousands of others, to await the outcome of the high level conference. I managed to secure a place in the courtyard, but countless citizens found themselves crowded outside the palace walls, or perched perilously on the remains of neighboring rooftops. A sea of torches illuminated the multitude.

The mellow light treated Aphrodisia favorably. She'd located a fresh gown and cleaned herself up a bit. She was in a merry mood, too, which I found out of keeping with the grim realities. I believed I knew the reason for her gaiety. She was constantly pinching my cheek or squeezing my hand. I did my best to ignore it.

The barbarians of Conax the Chimerical—several hundred fiercely-furred brutes in all—had established themselves in one quarter of the courtyard. Here they built fires from pieces of imperial furniture. At the moment they were roasting meat on spits and drinking themselves into insensibility. Where they found meat to cook, I preferred not to inquire!

The citizens stayed well away from these warriors, because now and then, some ferocious fellow would rise, begin to beat his breast and shoot out challenging glances.

Seated near me on the palace steps, Conax the Chimerical looked admiringly on this bravado. Like his painted furies, he seemed sullen and restive.

At last the remaining half of one palace door opened on sagging hinges. Bearded Babylos appeared, followed by His Splendor, Her Radiance, His Subservience, and several other blue beings to whom I had not been introduced. The multitude greeted Babylos with huzzahs. I applauded only politely, unable to quell a jealous twinge.

Babylos stilled the mob with upraised hands.

"My fellow Atlanteans! The freedom from tyranny and misrule which we have so long craved has been won—but for

136

high price. The Island Kingdom is bankrupt. And most of it lies in ruins. Putting those unhappy circumstances out of mind, let us face the future with a positive attitude. I have spent the afternoon discoursing with their excellencies, the members of the royal house of Zorop. Their world is much like ours, though it lies far across the heavens—"

Superstitious mutterings, then. And many signs against the evil eye. All were not as familiar as I with the stunning cosmology revealed by the Zorophim.

"—From these counsels, we have found a happy solution. We—the Atlanteans—have been invited, one and all, to migrate to the 'planet' Zorop. There, I am convinced, we will be well-received, granted status as free citizens, and be able to live our lives peacefully and democratically. On the morrow, we shall erect ballot boxes for a public vote. I urge a yes vote to the migration proposal, since I believe that, in order to survive, most of us would have to leave fair Atlantis anyway. Why not go in comfort? True, it means an awesome journey across vast 'interstellar space.' But that journey, His Splendor assures me, will be eminently safe. He has also made a quick head count. Due to the large number of Zorophimian vessels of exploration—vessels even now hovering out of sight in the heavens—all Atlanteans can be accommodated. Therefore what say you, citizens?"

With no more information than that, the populace burst into ecstatic cheers! Which only goes to show the dreadful manipulative powers of popular politicians! Call me a cynic, but I believed I knew the real reason for the generous offer of the Zorophim.

Conax, however, didn't go along with the majority.

"There'll be no Chimerians aboard your hell-spawned ships! We mean to return to our homeland—and continue our supremacy in pillage and plunder."

To this, his minions shouted agreement.

Babylos, however, was ready for the quibble.

"I'm afraid, your highness, that if the vote tomorrow is yes, you and your fellows will be required to accept it. Despite your superior fighting ability, you and your butch—ah, warriors are outnumbered by the populace. You could, if necessary, be put down, now that your advantage of surprise is gone. However, let's be reasonable! On Zorop, you'll be allowed to retain your title and perquisites. Further, His Splendor plans to put you in complete charge of the army."

"Complete charge?"

137

"Complete and utter. A challenging responsibility, wouldn't you say?"

"Um—well—it's worth thinking about."

Being not without some sense of proportion, he ultimately agreed to the bargain.

Poor fellow, he didn't discover till much later that the function of the army on Zorop was a hollow one; indeed, there had been no army at all until his coming, for peace was universal. By the time he made that unhappy finding, though, he had a conflict of somewhat different nature on his hands!

His Splendor glided to my side, placing a friendly hand on my arm. But I can tell a wheedling touch every time, no matter what celestial sphere saw its origin!

"Naturally, Vintner," said the blue king, "since we offer your fellow citizens the means of survival, we trust you will repay the gesture and bring with you on the journey—ah—certain valuable objects—"

"Vines to grow the Sacred Fuel? I thought that would be part of the bargain!"

"But of course."

"I suppose I might be able to do that. I presume my intimate knowledge of the Fuel will entitle me to a high post at your court?"

"Most assuredly," he returned. "A splendid residence, too. Plus a handsome stipend to defray expenses."

"Done!"

I confess the decision came as a relief. Perhaps, at long last, I might be free of hand-to-mouth existence. Become a vintner in deed as well as word.

And I certainly wasn't getting any younger! If I had to change careers—not to mention places of residence!—this seemed an ideal time.

Of course the plebiscite passed the next day, Babylos personally counting the pebble-boxes.

He announced the results right before sunset, to more enthusiastic cheering by the multitude. In truth, we Atlanteans have always been a flexible people, quick to find an advantage in an apparent defeat.

A holiday mood prevailed during the next few days, as small bundles of possessions were packed—the Zorophim had decreed a maximum weight allowance per person—and preparations for departure went forward.

I busied myself with the arbor cuttings, each of which I

carefully packed in earth-balls and burlap. None too healthy in my own garden, they would—I hoped!—manage to flourish on Zorop.

One disappointing circumstance intruded as citizens made ready for the leave-taking. Through Babylos, we were informed that the Zorophim didn't wish others of our kind to know anything about the migration. They tried to be polite about it. Yet it was clear they didn't think much of our race. They wanted no traffic with our "planet," save for that which had already transpired.

After some sharp bargaining long into the night, Babylos came up with another inspired solution. Atlantis must seem to have been destroyed by some mysterious tragedy!

Thus, on a clear, sun-drenched morning at the beginning of the month of the Eager Virgin, in the year of the Warty Toad, the wondrous iridescent ships of the Zorophim descended.

One by one they accepted their quota of Atlanteans—wicked Mimmo; swollen Rhomona; one-eyed Menos—all were going.

Many wept as they took farewell looks at their beloved Island Kingdom. But most seemed cheerful and optimistic.

As soon as one vessel had loaded, it lifted from the palace courtyard to make way for another. I discovered there had been a sort of lottery among the captains. The losers—two—were forced to transport the Chimerical horde. These worthies, I later learned, tried to build cook-fires of the ship furnishings, and insisted upon taking swims in the Sacred Fuel, until orders from Conax put a stop to it.

My cuttings and I went aboard the last vessel but one; the imperial flagship, as it turned out. And why not? Wasn't I a person of some substance?

As I boarded, a tear moistened my eye. Farewell, O noble island of my birth!

Hiding my sorrow, I took my place in the forward control compartment.

The captain, His Subservience, caused the craft to rise by manipulating several bizarre rods and levers. Another mysterious item of machinery was a kind of quartz crystal set into one wall. Its face produced a clear image of Atlantis growing smaller and smaller beneath us.

I studied the picture in the heart of the quartz, marveling at its clarity and detail. I was able to see the last Zorophimian

139

vessel. It hovered above members of the water works staff who were running along the top of the seawall.

The men darted down the public stairs at intervals, opening the great valves by turning the stone control wheels. Soon every last valve was ready to admit the sea, the moment high tide arrived.

My last image is a haunting one.

From our height, the Island Kingdom's destruction seemed less evident. Indeed, she sparkled like a gem in the midday sun. The water works officials clambered aboard their ship. It levitated promptly. Below it, breaking waves began to pour through the valves, inundating the streets and undermining the buildings. Slowly, my natal state began to sink.

Thus perished fair Atlantis!

I put my nose on Aphrodisia's shoulder and wept.

On the jeweled marvels of the vast heavenly abyss—"outer space," the Zorophim termed it—I shall not dwell overlong. I find that stylus-cramp has set in.

Besides, my main purpose in beginning this narrative, as the reader yet awake will recall, was to recount the true facts of the demise of Atlantis. This responsibility I trust I have discharged!

To sum up, we found voyaging with the Zorophim novel and agreeable. Only one last turn of fate lay in store.

This was revealed on our fourth night of voyaging.

A number of us sat at table in the king and queen's quarters, attemping to choke down a standard Zorophim meal consisting of a coarse cereal in a peculiar orange gravy. A remark by His Splendor caught my attention. He was telling Babylos about the centuries of peace on Zorop:

"—And, in addition, we have one universally honored rule which, in our opinion, contributes significantly to the maintenance of tranquility."

"What is it?" Conax barked, trying to avoid the playful fondlings of none other than Lady Voluptua.

To my astonishment, I had discovered her still alive after the holocaust. Evidently when Pytho dispatched her husband, she saw the handwriting on the wall. Thus, after the memorial service, she took up secret residence in the palace laundry, intending to come out only when she deemed it safe.

Now, the ex-queen seemed quite content, simply sitting next to Conax, whose thews her fingertips teased incessantly.

In response to the Chimerical one's brusque query, His Splendor said:

"The universal rule is this. Each citizen must have one, if not more, mates, preferably of the opposite sex. There are no exceptions."

I need not tell you what reaction that produced!

Aphrodisia at once began to caress me, and of course she made reference to my most recent promise of marriage.

"Come, Aphrodisia, unhand me! First of all, I'm not temperamentally suited for marriage, and never have been. Second, our business relationship is dissolved. You have no claim upon me there. Third, my promises were all made under duress. Indeed, I hardly even recall making them!"

His Splendor ticked a blue digit against the table.

"There are," he repeated, "no exceptions."

"Oh, thank you!" cried Aphrodisia. Obviously, I was in for it.

But there was worse to come!

"Vintner?" said the king.

"Yes?"

"From another of our vessels, we have received a message about you. A fellow citizen inquires after your welfare. A female named Swinnia. She also seems to have some claim on your affections."

"What, that wicked, obese nymph! How dare she—?"

Then I recalled certain other promises, likewise made in the heat of a desperate situation. I foresaw a grim reunion on Zorop—Aphrodisia on one hand, insisting she be my wife; Swinnia on the other, demanding to help me regain my manhood!

His Splendor, I'm sorry to say, found my plight amusing.

"You should be able to accommodate two mates, Hoptor. You're certainly big enough."

I could offer no reply. My gloom was only leavened by Lady Voluptua, who declared that she would mate with Conax.

His thews quivered in dismay, and he made some vague statement about being a free soul. Again, His Splendor said:

"No exceptions."

Conax looked utterly miserable. But at least I would not be the only one burdened with a nagging wife!

As we completed the sad meal, His Splendor took to musing aloud on recent experiences:

"—We can only remark again that most of the citizens of your little planet turned out to be a quarrelsome, superstitious lot. We have little hope for their progress. To allow

141

them to contaminate our existence on Zorop—no, do not scoff! It might be possible, after many generations. Even given their low mental order, they could conceivably learn to build craft similar to these. Why, they might even attempt to reach our planet! That would of course be highly undesirable. So we have developed a security plan. From time to time, we shall send one or two vessels such as this on secret scouting missions to your world. We shall have them survey—from a safe distance!—the state of the art of interplanetary travel. As a matter of curiosity, it might also be interesting to know whether the Island Kingdom's fate is ever discovered. But all this, we repeat, must be done in strict secrecy, as we wish no further intercourse with your race. Present company again excepted!"

And so, reader, the narrative of Hoptor closes.

Bound for a new and unpredictable home, my future at the mercy of a few miserable grapevines, and faced with a double helping of domestic travail, I almost wished myself back in Atlantis—under water!

I tried to imagine the reaction of future generations, upon seeing mysterious flashes in the sky—glowing discs whizzing every which way at remarkable speeds. Those luckless watchers would never know the true facts, unless one who was privy to them duly reported.

Thus, I end with an instruction.

Should the chronicle of Hoptor somehow survive—though given my present circumstances, I can't fathom how!—and should phantasmal lights appear in the heavens, do not be unduly alarmed.

The lights are merely the Zorophim, watching.

Should any question the origins of this statement, feel free to mention my name.